SECONDHAND DAYLIGHT

9/13

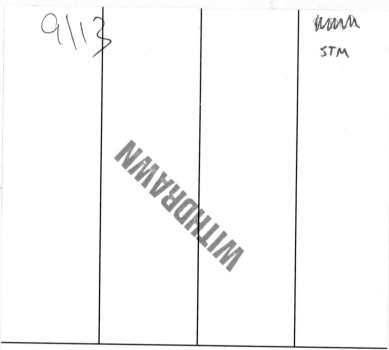

 STM

Please return on or before the latest date above.
You can renew online at *www.kent.gov.uk/libs*
or by telephone 08458 247 200

SECONDHAND DAYLIGHT

A James Ross mystery

D.J. Taylor

WINDSOR
PARAGON

First published 2012
by Corsair,
an imprint of Constable & Robinson Ltd
This Large Print edition published 2013
by AudioGO Ltd
by arrangement with
Constable & Robinson Ltd

Hardcover   ISBN: 978 1 4713 1294 6
Softcover   ISBN: 978 1 4713 1295 3

British Library Cataloguing in Publication Data available

Printed and bound in Great Britain by
TJ International Limited

For John Mullin

I enter the room
Confident enough
For now I tread
A straight and narrow way
So I sleep soundly
A little blue in the face
Cut-out shapes
In secondhand daylight

HOWARD DEVOTO

CONTENTS

ROSS, James Alexander Courtenay. b. 23.11.99. Mountstuart's (1913–17). Clerk, Headquarters, Southern Command, 1918. Trainee, Aberconway & Sons, Chartered Accountants, Hove, 1920. Secretary to the Hon. Clarence Dawlish MP, 1923–25. Assistant master, Croydon Technical School, 1927–28. Life guard, Brixton Lido, 1929. Travelling representative, Abraxas Carpet Cleaning Co., Holborn, 1931. *Publications*: 'You Can't Take It With You' in Alec Waugh, ed. *Georgian Stories of 1926*; *Words on a Dusty Page* (poems), 1928. Contributions to *New Statesman and Nation*, *Life and Letters*, *John O'London's Weekly*, *London Mercury* &c. Present whereabouts: unknown.

St Paul's School Old Boys' Record

PROLOGUE

'To be perfectly honest, we don't get many of your sort in here.'

'My sort being?'

'Well . . . people with some kind of education.'

'Plenty of public schoolboys on the PAC, surely?' I said. 'Newspapers go on about nothing else.' There was a still a blank-ish look on his face, so I breezed on: *'When the gates of Eton College closed behind the Hon. Algy Clutterbuck, few could have predicted that the man they called "The Toast of Pont Street" would soon be pawning his top hat for the price of a night's lodging.'*

'That's as may be,' the little bloke said, twiddling a pencil furiously between his fingers. 'Only they don't tend to come in here.'

It was one of those dull mornings in early autumn, with the rain clattering against the window like so many tin tacks, and I was sitting in an interview room at the Labour Exchange round the back of Shaftesbury Avenue. Not that you could see the rain, of course—the interview room was one of those daylight-free boxes, painted up in a shade of yellowy brown that reminded me of the Old Lady's cairn terriers—but the sound of it drummed all the way along the corridor. Quite what I was doing in the interview room I hadn't yet twigged. They were easy-going at the Shaftesbury Avenue Labour and usually stamped your card like a tallyman presented with a ten-bob note, but on this particular morning one of the chaps had hauled me out of the line,

1

taken me off to his cubby hole, found my name in a box file, offered me a cigarette—they were good cigarettes, too, Sahib Virginia Straight Cut at ninepence the packet—and suggested that we had a little chat. Now, I've been suspicious of little chats ever since Sergeant-Major Blatherwaite wanted to know what had become of the Mess Fund Subscription List, but he seemed a decent sort, and in any case it never pays to get on your high horse at the Labour.

'Mind if I ask you a few questions, Mr Ross?' He was a timid little black-haired chap, but with an odd look in his eye, like a Methodist elder up from Abertawe for the day walking past the ladies' underwear displays in Bourne & Hollingsworth's window.

'Fire away.'

'All right then. Age last birthday?'

Well, that wasn't a proposition from Euclid. 'Thirty-three,' I said. 'Thirty-four this November.'

'Any military experience?'

'Postal clerk at Southern Command headquarters, March to November 1918.' It had been censoring the Flanders mail, you'll understand, while Corporal Bannister brewed endless cups of strong tea and stared hopelessly out of the grille-window at passing VADs.

'Married man, are you?'

Now there'd been one or two close shaves, at least with Netta before that time she'd thrown the ring at me in the theatre queue, but there was no need to let on about any of this.

'Never had the pleasure,' I said.

'Last permanent address?'

'Actually,' I said, lifting my voice up a tone or

2

two, 'I've been staying at my mother's residence in Kent.' It's my experience that 'residence' is a better word to use than 'house', and sure enough the little bloke's eyes virtually gleamed. You could just see that he thought I'd been at some moated grange, rather than the Old Lady's bungalow at Tenterden with the cairn terriers moulting all over the drugget and both bars on.

'Any recent work experience?'

The noise of the rain was diminishing now, and the smell of the Sahib Virginia Straight Cut rose invitingly on the air, but the interview room still looked like the kind of place where someone had recently hung himself. Over the past few years I'd 'pursued a variety of occupations', as the Old Lady invariably put it in letters to relatives—I'd taught fretwork in a boys' school, sold carpet-cleaning lotion door-to-door and even officiated as secretary to the president of the Kensington Flat Earth Society—but somehow I knew none of these would cut much ice.

'Actually,' I said, 'I'm a writer.'

'Oh yes?' I couldn't work out if the little chap with the black hair didn't believe me or was simply disapproving. 'What sort of thing do you write?'

'Poems. Short stories.'

'Ever get anything published?'

'Just last week,' I said brightly, 'I had a piece printed in the *Blue Bugloss*.' The *Blue Bugloss* was super-refined, by the way, and had a list of words you weren't supposed to use in case the subscribers complained. 'Bugger' was one of them, and possibly 'balls'.

'I'm more of a *John O'London's* man myself,' the black-haired chap said. 'Never could get on with

3

some of that poetry. John Drinkwater, now that's my kind of poet. But the fact is a chap like you ought to be able to walk into a job, especially if he's not fussy.'

'Well, I'm not fussy,' I said. It was the truth as well. No one who's tried selling carpet-cleaning lotion door-to-door in Kensal Green on a wet Friday afternoon could ever be accused of being over-fastidious.

'How about this then?' he said, flicking a jellygraphed sheet of paper over the desk, where, I couldn't help noticing, someone had carved the words 'GRETA GARBO' with a penknife. There wasn't much more than a paragraph, saying that Mr Harold Samuelson of Dean Street W1 wanted a reliable, honest and hard-working young man of superior education to assist him in certain commercial undertakings on a part-time basis, remuneration and prospects excellent, accommodation thrown in.

'Sounds all right to me,' I said. 'What are "certain commercial undertakings"?'

'Rent collecting, isn't it?' the bloke said. 'Don't ask me why, but it's a tricky one to fill. We've sent half-a-dozen chaps down there since Christmas and none of them have suited. Make a go of this and you'll be doing me no end of a favour, I can tell you.'

'Don't mind trying,' I said. That's the thing about me: I've never minded trying.

'Who's this Mr Samuelson when he's at home?'

'Owns some sort of nightclub in Dean Street. Jewish, I'm afraid.'

'Oh well,' I said, getting up from my chair, and noticing that the sole of one of my shoes was about

4

to part company with the upper. 'Beggars can't be choosers.'

'Well, good luck then.'

'Thanks,' I said.

* * *

Outside the rain had all but stopped, and there were smeary streaks running down the corridor windows. There was a square of mirror on the wall next to a notice about men being wanted to build a municipal park bandstand up in Colindale and for some reason I stopped and took a squint. Half an inch under six feet, not bad-looking, with one of those honest, open faces that women think they can confide things to. A few too many things on occasion. And Sir Edward Marsh, —— him, had once said that a poem I'd had published in *Public School Verse* had showed 'enormous promise'. No doubt about it, I ought to have been able to stroll into any job worth the taking. Back in the main hall three serpentine queues of blokes in mackintoshes and flat caps with *Mirror*s under their arms trailed back from the grilles, and a man in a tam o'shanter and trousers that ended halfway down his calves was being quietly sick into a waste-paper basket. The little bloke with the black hair had been bang right: they didn't get many of my sort at the Shaftesbury Avenue Labour.

PART ONE

WARDOUR STREET

Soho girls in Wardour Street
Don't have time to chat
Late at night go home to Ealing,
Mothers, and the cat.

James Ross, Soho Eclogues

The sign on the wall just inside the door read MARITAL AIDS, but in fact there were none of these on display. Instead the shop sold secondhand copies of Marie Stopes's *Married Love* and Professor Silas Hergesheimer's *Man the Sexual Being*. There were also some packets of postcards and a cork-board on which artists' models offered their services at ten shillings an hour. Outside it was raining and there was a strong smell of tar. Mr Slattery, the establishment's proprietor, sat on a high stool by the cash register addressing one of his customers. Choosing his words with a certain amount of deliberation, he said:

'It's a good old life. You'd be surprised. I sometimes think I ought to give it up, take one of those cottages down on the coast everyone always talks about, Winchelsea way or Rye, but then I ask myself: what would I do there? If you're bound to a trade, you don't want to leave it. It stands to reason.'

There was no one else in the shop, which had a high, cavernous roof with a lime-green stain at its epicentre that informed judges sometimes said reminded them of the map of Greece. The smell of the tar, which came from some repairs to the pavement that had been completed earlier that morning, blended with the smoke from Mr Slattery's Camel cigarette and a surprisingly sinister reek of damp. Some of the artists' models came as cheap as eight shillings. Mr Slattery said:

'You get all sorts. I don't know a trade that doesn't. I've got customers who don't come in here from one month to the next, but they know where to find me when they do. People tell me I ought to advertise more, make a show of it, but that's not the way. Start making a song and dance and you only get a lot of riff-raff through the door. That's what I always say.'

The repairs to the pavement had not been extensive, but a small area of the newly gleaming tarmacadam had been closed off and a series of ropes strung between trestles. From the top of the near-most trestle a workman's lamp winked intermittently. Towards the back of the shop the goods were more miscellaneous, almost extending to bric-a-brac. Here there were such items as antique Coronation mugs, a jigsaw of HMS *Hood* in dry dock and a cuckoo clock with a defective spring. Mr Slattery said:

'Of course the police come by now and again. I don't mind. They've got a job to do just like anyone else. Besides, they're very friendly. It's not like the old days. Why, when Lord Byng was commissioner they'd be in here every day to look at the books. There was one constable read a copy of *The Plumed Serpent* from cover to cover. I had to make him a cup of tea while he did it. We used to make a joke

10

of it. It's not like that now.'

Outside the rain had become to come down harder. A hearse went by, drawn by horses whose manes had been dyed so many times they seemed almost purple. Mr Slattery took an orange out of the till, where it lurked between a couple of five-pound notes and a roll of elastic bands, and began desultorily to peel it. He said:

'I'm not saying Soho doesn't need to have an eye kept on it. No indeed. There's some people think we're all libertines and demireps. It's not true. Why, when I heard Mrs Meyrick was dead I said to Dulcie that does for me: "If people knew the harm that woman had done they wouldn't be so sentimental about her and saying she was taken before her time."'

It was a very pungent orange, and Mr Slattery was careful to hold it away from his face as he peeled it. The hearse had gone by now, although the sound of the horses' hoofs could still be heard further down the street. In its wake trailed a small collection of mourners: girls with shawls over their heads; ancient women, their faces apparently lined with the dust of centuries, in dark costumes; squat, mustachioed men with olive-eyed children riding on their arms. Mr Slattery looked suddenly lugubrious, ground down, as if he wanted to rush out into the street, throw himself at the mourners' feet and rend the air with his cries. But the mood passed. He said:

'Those Italians always make a fuss of their funerals. I can't say I understand why. Whenever I've buried anyone I always wanted to get it over as quick as possible. The fondest farewells are the briefest. That's what I've always said.'

Mr Slattery looked up. The shop was empty and the orange was gone. He rolled the fragments of peel into a little ball and swept them into the wastepaper basket with the flat of his hand. Queer how often that happened. But it couldn't be helped. There was a copy of Priestley's *Angel Pavement* lying in the alcove at the back, next to the balls of darning wool and the *John McCormack Songbook*. He could read a couple of chapters before he went and got his lunch. Outside the rain was easing and the funeral procession had turned the corner into Noel Street. Mr Slattery, who had once in his youth been on some unimaginable journey to the countryside beyond Turin, had a sudden memory of olive groves, a basket piled high with corks, prosciutto lying curled up on a plate.

There was a snick as the door of the shop sprang open and a customer came in: a little man in a trilby with the corner of his coat pulled up to his face. Mr Slattery took no notice of him. Instead he said, 'Good morning. Please feel free to browse. All the magazines are for sale. Specialist items towards the back.' The boom of his voice—he had sung tenor in a Methodist church choir as a young man—echoed off the cavernous ceiling and he fell silent. The little man ignored this invitation, but picked out a copy of *The Young Man's Guide to Marriage* and started leafing through it. Mr Slattery liked customers who looked you in the eye and returned a greeting. Civility, in fact. He had the copy of *Angel Pavement* open next to the till now, so that one or two fragments of orange pulp threatened to despoil its royal blue covers.

Miss Matfield had gone to Hays Wharf to take

12

down some letters for Mr Golspie as he sat in the saloon of the *Lemmala*, awaiting transfer to the Baltic. *London was really marvellous, and the wonder of it rushed up in her mind and burst there like a rocket, scattering a multi-coloured host of vague but rich associations, a glittering jumble of history and nonsense and poetry, Dick Whittington and galleons, Muscovy and Cathay, East Indiamen, the doldrums far away, and the Pool of London, lapping here only a stone's throw from the shops and offices and buses.* Good old London, thought Mr Slattery, who was fifty-seven, with a bottle nose and two chins, and as unromantic a figure as it was possible to conceive; now there was a subject. There was another snick at the door and a second man came into the shop: taller than the first, and not so seedy-looking, but apparently having some connection with him as the two of them went and conferred over the display copies of *Beauty, Health and Nature* which the police had taken such an interest in on their last visit.

Olive groves basking in the sun. J. B. Priestley. The Pool of London. *Beauty, Health and Nature*. Mr Slattery thought that he needed cheering up. Worse, the gramophone shop next door was having one of its demonstrations, and he could hear music coming through the wall.

> *Tonight I'm alone, broken-hearted*
> *To mother I've murmured 'Goodbye-ee'*
> *From the home of my youth I've departed*
> *With a tear in my bonny blue eye.*

There was another smell leaching into the air to add to the compound of tar, damp, orange peel and cigarette. Mr Slattery thought it was burning and wondered where it was coming from. The two men had their heads bent together at the corner of the display in such a way that it partly obscured the rest of their bodies, and Mr Slattery thought he ought to go and see what they were doing. It was definitely the smell of burning, he thought. Nellie Wallace's voice—high, cracked, confiding—continued to buzz through the wall:

> *Forget all my troubles I can't, tho' I've tried*
> *There's only one thing left for*
> *me—sui-ci-hi-hide*
> *I don't like my mother's pie-crust*
> *Eat it? No! I'd sooner die fust!*

A part of him was still with Miss Matfield as she got out of the taxi in Tooley Street, negotiated the labyrinth of winding lanes and came at last to the ship, sequestered and romantic, on which Mr Golspie sat hatching his ineffable schemes. 'May I help you, gentlemen?' he heard himself asking vaguely. He discovered that the charring smell came from some copies of the *Naturists' Gazette* to which the taller of the two men was calmly holding his cigarette lighter. Fascinated despite himself, Mr Slattery watched them burn. The little man in the trilby hat, he noticed—and somehow the noticing was an effort, much less interesting than the smouldering pages of the *Naturists' Gazette*—was making his way to the till. Nellie Wallace's voice seemed to be coming from a long way off, like the voice of an Arctic explorer cut off by the sudden, pulverizing descent of snow:

14

I've tied it round me neck, and tomorrow I shall be—
Down at the bottom of the deep blue sea.

'Hi there!' Mr Slattery said. 'You can't . . .' But the other man had reached out and sent a shelf-full of books bustling into movement. Like a row of dominoes they rippled back on top of each other and then tumbled, one after another, onto the threadbare carpet. There was beauty in it, Mr Slattery thought distractedly, strong, terrible beauty. When the little man's hand went into the till, his first thought was for the other orange he had hidden there next to the elastic bands, and the hank of cotton wool for whenever his ear ached. Somewhere—a long way off, it seemed—a window broke. Mr Slattery lay on the carpet, where it was cooler and the smell of burning—a whole case of magazines was on fire now—seemed less oppressive. Nellie Wallace had fallen silent. They left the shop laughing, passers-by scattering in their wake, feet careening through the fresh tar.

2

THE GIRL IN
THE SECOND FLOOR BACK

Sergeant Snooks on Meard Street corner
Soho's particular dragon
Pockets are full of ten-bob watches
Nabbed from drunks in the wagon

James Ross, Soho Eclogues

Fact is, I always remember the time it all started—Gladys, and the club being smashed up and the night in the cells in West End Central—seeing that it was the day the letters came. I'd just come down the stairs from my digs and was standing on the doorstep looking out into Rathbone Place and wondering if the packet of Woodbines in the lining of my mac was empty or not when a postman came barging over from the other side of the street and stuck a couple of envelopes into my hand. It was one of those damp, cold mornings you get at the end of October, with the Post Office lorries headed for the depot in Rathbone Street spraying last night's rain over the pavement as they barrelled by, and what with the letters, and badly wanting to sit down again and smoke the fag I was pretty sure was left in the packet, I decided I'd let work hang for the next twenty minutes or so and go and have breakfast in Lew Levy's caff.

As it turned out I was wrong about the fag, but by the time I'd collected my coffee and two slices and picked up a *Sketch* that someone had left under one of the chairs the rain had come on again and I reckoned I was better off where I was. There were a couple of tarts moving beyond the plate-glass window, and I watched them clatter over the pavement to the awning above the butcher's shop, showing more leg than was decent, tried a sip of Lew Levy's coffee—which wasn't too bad, for all it was made of chicory essence—and then took a squint at what Captain Tanqueray, who'd been my boss in the army, would have called my 'matutinal correspondence'.

The first letter, which was from Jimmy Carstairs, I'd been half expecting. It was a circular, jellygraphed onto hard, expensive paper that practically crackled under your fingers, and announced that Mr J. B. Carstairs was relinquishing his post as editor of the *Blue Bugloss* with immediate effect, to be replaced by Mr Harold Festing-Jones, author of *Attic Sojourns* and *In My Window Box*. At the bottom, Jimmy had written: *Dear James, Sorry to leave you in the s—t. Come and look me up next time you're in Teddington. I'll put in a word with Harold.* So that was another connection gone west. As for Harold printing any of my stuff, a virgin had more chance of preserving her honour in the harem of Haroun El-Rashid.

As for the second letter, which had been sent on from the Old Lady's in Tenterden, well I'd been half expecting that too. It went:

Dear James,

There is no point in your telephoning me as you did last Sunday, because on the next occasion

17

that you do so I shall certainly refuse to speak to you. I repeat that no earthly good can ever come of our seeing each other again, and that I was a fool to listen to the things you said. You may keep the Somerset Maugham book as I doubt that, in the circumstances, I could ever bear to look at it again.

I am sending this from my aunt's house in Scotland, where I have gone to recover from what has been a very trying experience. I strongly advise you not to attempt to contact me there—or anywhere else.

Netta

What do you do on these occasions? I'd had run-ins with Netta before, of course, but this looked as if it really was the order of the bowler hat. For a moment I wondered about taking the express up to Auchtermuchty or wherever it was she was staying and turning up out of the blue on the aunt's doorstep, but then I remembered that I'd left the address at the Old Lady's. Besides, I wouldn't get paid until Friday and there was eighteen bob owing at the laundry. No, I'd just have to cut my losses.

Curiously enough, I didn't feel so bad after that. Outside it was still raining—the tarts were hunkered down under the butcher's awning comparing the ladders in their stockings—so I finished my coffee, ate the two slices and read a story in the *Sketch* about a man who'd been swallowed by a whale somewhere in the Middle East and then spat out two days later still alive but bleached white by its gastric juices. Then I thought about Jimmy again, and why on earth he'd wanted

18

to give up the *Blue Bugloss*, with its comfy chairs and its Roedean-accented secretaries for scripting quota-quickies down in Teddington. There are some of us, you see, who're prepared to suffer for our art.

*   *   *

What with the rain keeping up, and thinking about Netta and all the poems I wouldn't be writing for the *Blue Bugloss*, it was twenty to eleven by the time I came out into Rathbone Street and I reckoned I'd best be hurrying on sharpish. It was only my third day in the job, you see, and I didn't want word getting back to Sammy that I'd been swinging the lead. The rain had been replaced by a weak sun, the colour of a very pale fried egg, but there were still clouds away over the heath, which meant that some poor b——r in Hampstead who'd gone out minus his overcoat was properly getting it. I'd got the notebook in my hand by now, and as I trekked south across Oxford Street into Soho I took a dekko at the day's beat, which was the Meard Street–Brewer Street, with a finish off in Glasshouse Street and, if I could manage it, a cut off the joint and two veg. at the Denmark Arms.

Meard Street, where I fetched up five minutes later, nearly colliding with a sad-faced old chap with a sandwich board saying THE END OF THE WORLD IS NIGH, smelled of cats' meat from the stall at the far end, and I leaned up against a lamp post while I tried to find the right place in the book. The first house wasn't one of Sammy's, as it turned out, but the second one went:

19

FFF—Mrs Wisbeach
FFB—Mr Sibierski*
SFF—Vacant
SFB—Miss Marlborough**

The asterisks, as I'd already discovered, meant that there was more than a fortnight owing. Fact is, I've no self-consciousness about knocking on people's doors and dunning them for rent, so once I got my bearings I fairly sprinted up the staircase and gave a rat-a-tat-tat on the door of the first floor front that was fit to raise the dead. After a long while, just as I was wondering whether I ought to repeat the knock, there was a kind of shuffling noise a long way off, and then, quite unexpectedly given how far away the shuffling seemed to be coming from, the door swung open.

'Yes?'

She was a little, thin, dried-up old lady with grey-to-brindling hair gathered up under a lace cap, and a fox terrier snapping at her ankles.

'Mrs Wisbeach?'

'That's right.' She gave me one of those vague looks which I remembered the Old Lady reserving for people who came round collecting subs for the Tenterden Trefoil Guild. 'Are you the man from the baker's?'

'No, I'm Mr Ross. I've called about the rent.'

'You'd better come in. Down Hercules!' The latter was to the fox terrier, which was nosing excitably at my trouser bottoms. 'He hasn't been himself all morning,' she went on. 'It's that pussy's butcher.'

'Pussy's who?'

20

'The cats' meat stall at the end of the street. He gets the scent of it, you see, when I open the kitchen window. Would you like a cup of tea?'

It's always been my experience that old ladies like respectful heartiness, so I nodded my head and practically clicked my heels together. 'It would be a pleasure, Mrs Wisbeach.'

Pretty soon we were in a kind of sitting room, with an old horsehair sofa and a couple of armchairs, which looked as if Hazlitt had slept on them before he quit the place in 1817, and a mahogany mantelpiece dominated by a photograph of an old boy with a bald head and mutton-chop whiskers. The fox terrier was still nosing around at my turn-ups, but I gave it a tap with my instep that sent it sliding a foot or so over the carpet. As it turned out Mrs Wisbeach had lost interest in Hercules. She was staring at the photograph of the old boy on the mantelpiece.

'My late husband,' she said.

'When did he die?'

'Oh he didn't die, Mr Ross.'

'Didn't he?'

'No. That is not an expression which I care to use.'

The fox terrier had got back on its legs now, and was regarding me a bit more warily.

'Isn't it?'

'No. My husband *passed on*.' There was a pause. 'Into the *majority*.'

'I see.'

While she was in the kitchen I had another squint around the room. This contained, in addition to a phonograph which looked as if Noah had spent his time listening to it on the Ark, a jam jar stuffed with threepenny bits, a copy of *John O'London's Weekly* and a glass-fronted bookcase full of books with titles like *Spirit Hands Have Touched Me* and *Whispers From the Abyss*. I'd taken one out and was staring at a picture of a chap's hand suspended over what looked like a hank of butter muslin when Mrs Wisbeach came back with the tea.

'Are you interested in spiritualism, Mr Ross?'

It seemed a shame to disappoint the old girl, so I said, 'Up to a point, Mrs Wisbeach.'

'A fellow-voyager in the dear dead lands beyond recall?'

'Naturally one wants to know about the people who've . . . passed on.'

'And yet the membrane that separates us from them is so very permeable.'

It was about half past eleven now, and I knew that if I didn't hurry things along I wasn't going to make the Denmark Arms. 'About the rent, Mrs Wisbeach?'

'Oh yes, the rent,' she said. 'How much is it?'

'Twenty-eight shillings, Mrs Wisbeach.'

'It does seem rather a lot.'

I consulted the list Sammy had given me. 'Twenty-eight shillings is what it says here.'

'No, I mean considering the look of the place. Not to mention the fixtures. I've written to Mr Samuelson three times about it and never had a reply. I think it's disgraceful.' The fox terrier had slunk away and was playing—a touch disconsolately—with an elastic band. 'Come and look at this.'

We went into the kitchen and inspected a window–frame that had started to rot and an overflow pipe that Mrs Wisbeach said leaked. The larder door was open, and while we were doing this I counted the tins of beetroot she had in it. There were seventeen of them.

'So you see,' Mrs Wisbeach said. 'Twenty-eight shillings and never a bit of consideration. I'd go and stay with my sister-in-law in Reigate, only the beds are never properly aired.'

'It does seem rather bad. Perhaps I should speak to Mr Samuelson.'

'You seem a nice young man. Not at all like some of the other people who've come collecting. Would you like another cup of tea?'

'I really should be on my way, Mrs Wisbeach. Now, about the rent . . .'

'I think I should only give you fifteen shillings this week, Mr Ross, seeing that you're going to speak to Mr Samuelson.'

The first rule of rent-collecting, according to Sammy, was that you should always aim to come away with something. Besides, the tea had been A1—real Pekoe Points from the bottom of the pot. Anyhow, I was just tearing out a receipt from the book, and thinking that if Hercules came near me again he'd get it somewhere in the foreleg this time, when a thought seemed to strike her and she said, 'If you would care to join us next Tuesday evening, Mr Ross, I'm sure you would find it to your advantage.'

Was she getting up a bridge four? Showing her holiday snaps? There was no way of telling.

'What for, exactly?'

'There are a group of us—like-minded souls, you understand—who seek to penetrate . . . beyond the veil.'

'You mean a seance?'

'I would not put it so vulgarly. Let us say that there are ways in which the majority may be . . . approached.'

Well, I knew Sammy wouldn't want that thirteen bob standing over for very long, so I handed the receipt over with a flourish that would have done credit to a duke's butler.

'It sounds very interesting.'

'You would like to come?'

'Certainly.'

'Goodbye then, Mr Ross.' We were back in the hallway by now, underneath a particularly grim representation of Lincoln Cathedral. 'I can't think what's the matter with Hercules. He's usually so boisterous.'

Well, I could have told her. Thirty seconds later I was out on the landing again with a ten-bob note and two half-crowns in my trouser pocket, banging on the door of the first floor back. There was no reply, although I could hear a radio playing 'A Wandering Minstrel I', which spooked me a bit as it was something Netta had liked. While I stood there I wondered how I was going to get out of Mrs Wisbeach's Tuesday night at-home. In any case, it was evens she'd realize I was only being polite, surely? The radio had been switched off by now and there was a noise of someone walking about. In cases like this you were supposed to hang about on the QT in the hope that they'd then open the door to see if you'd gone, but it was a quarter to twelve now and all I had to show for the morning so far was Mrs Wisbeach's fifteen bob, so I hared up the staircase, ignored the second floor front, which was being redecorated and had its door propped open with a chamber pot, and thumped on the knocker

24

of the second floor back.

'Yes?'

She must have been about twenty-six or twenty-seven, blonde and green-eyed, with her hair done up in papers and a dressing gown pulled tight over what looked like a pair of silk pyjamas, and you didn't have to be a particularly astute observer of the female sex to work out that she was either just going to take a bath or had just finished taking it.

'Good morning, madam. I've called about the rent.'

'You don't look like Leslie. What happened to him?'

'He had to go away.'

In fact, according to Sammy, no one had a clue where Leslie had gone. It takes all sorts, I suppose.

'That's a pity. I liked Leslie.'

I was getting used to the green eyes now, which gave off a powerful stare. There was a clump of face powder on her chin which hadn't come off in the wash. Over her shoulder pale yellow light showed a half-open door, and there was a dress laid out on an ironing board and a couple of beer bottles on a stool. All this flummoxed me somehow, and I had to take another squint at the book before I could remember her name.

'Miss Marlborough?'

'Call me Gladys. Most of the collectors do. You'd better come in.'

In the space behind the door my foot collided with something soft and yielding. It turned out to be half a loaf of bread. Gladys picked it up and put it on a ledge by the door frame, next to a copy of *Film Pictorial* on whose cover Stanley Logan said how much he'd liked being in *Havana Widows* with Joan

Blondell and a picture postcard of the Eiffel Tower. She said, 'This place is awfully squalid.'

'It's not so bad.'

'No, I mean the building. Did you know there's bracket fungus growing out of the wall in the spare room? Not to mention the mice. You ought to do something about it.'

'I'll speak to Mr Samuelson.'

We'd be reserving the smoking room at the Garrick for my next chat with Sammy, I thought, if this went on much longer. Meanwhile, I was still trying to get the hang of Gladys, who clearly enjoyed dining off cans of sardines—there was one half-open on the windowsill with a fork sticking out of it—but whose dressing gown couldn't have cost less than ten guineas. Still, there's no accounting for taste. I'd once seen Mrs Bence-Jones, back in the accountancy days at Hove, eat chicken *à l'impératrice* off a page torn out of the *Morning Post*.

'Not much of a job,' she said, as we came into the sitting room. 'Collecting people's rents, I mean.'

'All I could get.'

'What do you usually do?'

'Stories, mostly. Poems. In the magazines.'

'I met a writer once,' she said.

'Who was that then?'

'Said his name was Squire. He came in the club one evening. I think Mr Rappaport threw him out.'

'Is that where you work?'

'What?'

'In a nightclub?'

'That'd be telling. Anyway, I thought you came about the rent. How much is it?'

I consulted the oracle. 'Three weeks at twenty-eight shillings. That's four pounds four.'

'You'd better sit down while I have a look.'

Fact is, I've been in a fair few girls' sitting rooms in my time, and this didn't fit the type by a long chalk. There was a bunch of roses going brown on the sofa, together with a card from somebody called Dennis, and a pile of underwear stacked up on one of the chairs, beneath a photograph of Victor Maclagan inscribed 'To Gladys with best love'. While I was getting my bearings, Gladys went round searching in odd drawers, grubbed up a copper or two off the carpet and then produced a couple of fur coats and began going through the pockets. There was a clattering noise above our heads and I jerked my eye up instinctively at the ceiling.

'It's the pigeons,' she explained. 'They get in through the slates.'

'How do they get out again?'

'I don't know. Why should I care? I expect they just die there.'

There was a pile of coins on the card table by this time, and she whipped through them like a croupier with a stack of roulette chips. I stared at the roses, which were from one of the posh shops in Regent Street, and wondered about Dennis and whether he'd got to sit on Gladys's sofa next to the heap of smalls and the photo of Victor Maclagan. That's the kind of thing I think about in situations like this, which just goes to show, I suppose.

'Seventeen and eightpence,' she said eventually. 'It won't do, will it?'

'Couldn't you borrow some more?'

'Who from? The girls at the club are all saving up to get married. Or if they're not saving up to get married, then they're saving up to get divorced.'

There was a smell coming up from the floor below which could have been boiled haddock. 'I say,' she said, after another skim through the pile of coins on the card table, 'the rent will have to stand. You couldn't lend me a pound could you?'

Could I? There was nine bob left to last me till Friday, and this was only Wednesday morning. Then I had a brainwave. If I took Mrs Wisbeach's fifteen bob and put in five of my own, that would make it up to a quid. It would mean making some excuse about Mrs Wisbeach, but the way I looked at it there were two distinct advantages. I'd have her undying gratitude, and I could say that I had to have it back before the next rent day, which might mean I could get to see her somewhere other than Meard Street.

'I could let you have a pound,' I said. 'But I'd want it back by Tuesday.'

'You're a sport.' She'd taken a packet of fags off the table—De Reszke they were, none of your cheap brands—and stuck one in the corner of her mouth. 'I get paid Friday night, you see, and there's always tips over the weekend.'

I thought I'd chance my arm a bit, so I said, 'Do you know the Café Polska in Berwick Street?'

She nodded, without looking too enthusiastic.

'I could meet you there Tuesday afternoon,' I said. 'About two o'clock.'

She was drawing on the cigarette in angry little 'psts'. 'All right then.'

I flicked my hand in the direction of the bunch of roses. 'Won't Dennis mind?'

'Dennis! As if *he'd* care.'

'Two o'clock Tuesday then.'

'All right.'

28

Twenty seconds later I was out on the landing and nearly colliding with a mousetrap and a pile of *News Chronicle*s that someone had left in a heap. There was the sound of a radio coming from the first floor back, but somehow I didn't fancy knocking again—I had an idea that Sibierski, if that was who it was, was a dab hand at this particular game—so I breezed off down the staircase and back into Meard Street. Here the rain had come on again and there were rat-faced blokes with their shoulders hunched up inside their macs going in and out of the corner shops and vague women with umbrellas over their heads standing under street lamps—tarts, probably, but you can never tell.

By rights I should have carried on down the street—Sammy owned numbers 3 and 4, not to mention the boot and shoe concern at number 6— but somehow, what with the rain and the kick of getting a date with Gladys, I didn't feel like it. And after lending her five bob I knew I wasn't going to make lunch at the Devonshire Arms. As I saw it, the only place I'd get anything to eat was back at my digs in Rathbone Place, where I reckoned there might be half a loaf of bread and some cheese in the cupboard that the mice wouldn't have found. The rain was coming down in torrents by now, with the taxis sending up gouts of water as they went past, so I nipped into a tobacconist, paid twopence for a packet of five Park Drive and smoked the first of them as I walked down Wardour Street, past the poster that said Mosley would be talking about the Bolshevik Menace at the Farringdon Memorial Hall and the old chap with the row of fake war medals selling matches that nobody ever bought.

It hadn't been a bad morning, I thought,

despite the letters and the temporary loss of Mrs Wisbeach's fifteen shillings. Someone had chucked a brick through the window of the dirty bookshop at the far end of Wardour Street and there was a policeman in the doorway taking down addresses, but I was so wrapped up in Gladys, and the silk pyjamas, and the bunch of roses, and two o'clock Tuesday at Café Polska, that I barely gave it a thought. Crossing over Oxford Street a moment or two later, though, I noticed something odd. This was that someone had clearly been in such a hurry to get wherever he was going that he'd stepped into a pile of tarmacadam along the way. You could see footprints made out of black tar and little fragments of stone all the way over the road and into Rathbone Street. Even odder was the fact that they seemed to stop right outside my digs.

3

HOME AND ABROAD

At the old Blue Lantern they don't like yids
The Bag of Nails is on the skids
At the Embassy Club the company's mixed
The Kit-Kat's baccarat table is fixed.

James Ross, Soho Eclogues

'There's some people think running a nightclub's a piece of cake,' Mr Samuelson said. 'But I'm here to tell them different.'

'I can see that.'

'Take the hours now. An ordinary business chap can go home at six o'clock for his tea. Earlier, even. Some nights I've got to sit here until three o'clock in the morning. And the things that go on. Why, only last week one of the girls found the Honourable Miss Shepton-Marjoribanks having a fit in the ladies' powder room, and I had to telephone the Foreign Office and have her father come round and collect her.'

'It makes you think.'

'And then she had the cheek to send in a bill for cleaning a dress that one of the waiters had spilled hollandaise sauce on. I sent that straight back, I can tell you.'

We were sitting in Mr Samuelson's office at the Toreador, or rather Mr Samuelson was sitting and I was standing in the doorway, next to a picture of the Prince of Wales staring mournfully at a cocktail glass with about half a pound of fresh fruit dangling over its side that someone had just handed him. Outside in Dean Street the rain was coming down in sheets and, judging by the police van pulled up on the far side of the pavement, the Cadenza Gentleman's Club over the way was having one of its raids.

'I warned old Crewkerne to be careful about those cards he hands out,' Mr Samuelson said, seeing the van for the first time. 'Told him all that stuff about refined lady companions at reasonable rates wouldn't do.'

'Is that right?'

'There's people think that just because Jix has gone from the Home Office nobody cares about the Defence of the Realm Act any more. Well, they're wrong about that. Dead wrong.'

Somewhere above our heads there was a terrific shattering noise that sounded as if someone had dropped a stack of plates. All in all, it was just another ordinary afternoon at the Toreador. This was the second time I'd been in Sammy's office, which had clearly been fitted out by someone who'd seen one of those posters for Lalique glass. You couldn't move for little bowls and ashtrays that looked as if they'd been chiselled out of blocks of Turkish Delight. Plus there was one of those big roll-top mahogany desks you see in ads about thrusting young city types with firm handshakes and lantern jaws who're really pulling in the big dough, but which rather swamped Sammy, who was on the spindly side.

'And the worst of it,' Mr Samuelson said, sounding like a Belgrave Square dowager who's just discovered that Lady Kitty next door is getting her marmalade from the Co-op, 'is that it makes trouble for the rest of us.'

The Toreador, I'd quickly worked out, was a middling kind of club: not in the same league as the Embassy or the Kit-Kat, but several streets ahead of the Bag of Nails or the Blue Lantern in Ham Yard. Mr Samuelson, who owned it, and two dozen or so houses where I went round collecting the rent, was a thin, Jewish-looking bloke about three or four years older than me, who gave out that he'd been to Winchester but if you ask me had spent his formative years picking up fag ends in the Mile End Road. Still he was paying me three quid a week so I wasn't complaining. Interestingly enough, he'd turned out to be a pal of my lawyer chum Tommy Kilmarnock, who between you and me wasn't too particular about the company he kept.

'Anyhow,' Samuelson went on, waving his hand and sending a little cloud of coconut oil into the space between us, 'I'm sure you're aware of the situation we find ourselves in. Public school man, aren't you?'

'Indeed.'

'War service too, I'll be bound.'

Christ, I thought, he'll be putting me up for Brooks's if this goes on much longer. Plus, it was already 1.45, which meant that I'd only fifteen minutes until I was supposed to be meeting Gladys at the Polska—if she turned up, that is. I reckoned it might not be too good a scheme to tell him about the hut on the Downs where Corporal Hackett and I sat steaming open the mail, so I just nodded my head and murmured something about 'administrative duties'. It seemed to do the trick because he sent another great gust of hair oil

33

reeking in my direction and said: 'I was reserved occupation myself. Running a munitions factory in Shoreditch as a matter of fact. Couldn't be helped. But the point is, chaps like us ought to stick together.'

Curiously enough, I was hardly listening to him by this time. I was too busy thinking about Gladys and the fork sticking out of the sardine tin in the second-floor back at Meard Street. Wasn't there a poet who said the things we remember girls for are the mundane details, and if you really fancy someone it's the torn-up copy of *Old Moore's Almanac* in her waste-paper basket that'll stick. Lurking at the back of my head, too, was the memory of saying I'd go to Mrs Wisbeach's spirit-hands-have-touched-me. Besides, in my experience when people start talking about chaps like us sticking together it's time to count the spoons and make sure there's a clear route to the door. Anyhow, some of this seemed to have occurred to Sammy, because all of a sudden he looked a bit grim, stared at the pencil in his hand as if he wasn't quite sure how it had got there and shot another look out of the window, where a policeman was standing on the steps of the Cadenza talking to a sulky-looking redhead in a dressing gown. Then he said:

'To be perfectly frank, we're a bit short-handed in the evening. The waiters can't always be everywhere. You get people wandering around sometimes looking for a place to put their coats. I had a man come into my office last week and try to sell me an insurance policy. And then sometimes the cloakroom staff need an eye kept on them. I went in there the other night and found they'd got a spirit lamp from somewhere and were making themselves cups of tea. There won't be a great deal to do. It just needs a firm hand.'

'How long would I have to stay?'

'Only until midnight. We stop serving food then, and the girls start going off.'

Well, it didn't sound too bad an idea, and pretty soon I found myself signing up for three nights a week, hours from eight to twelve, and an extra two quid to add to the three I was getting for pounding the Meard Street staircases. It would mean taking my evening suit out of pawn, but Sammy muttered something about 'dress allowance' and subbed me a quid to be going on with, and two minutes later I was out in Dean Street thinking that the day hadn't started too badly after all. The rain had stopped and the police van had gone from outside the Cadenza, but the sulky redhead in the dressing gown was still standing on the front step with an unlit cigarette between her fingers and I caught her eye as I went past.

'Got a match?'

The correct thing to say in these circumstances was, 'Not since Valentino died,' but she was the kind of girl who looked as if she'd chew your head off if you gave her any chat, so I simply held open the packet of Swan Vestas and waited until she'd lit one.

'Spot of trouble?'

'You can say that again. Haven't seen so many coppers since the time they raided the Silver Slipper one Christmas just as they were doing the Cossack dance.'

'Any idea why?' I couldn't have cared less myself, but I had a notion that Sammy might like to know.

'Archdeacon's daughter that gave her dad the slip turned out to be working as an 'ostess. There was a story in the *Mirror*.'

As it happened I'd seen the piece myself. It was one of those stories that begin, *In a Herefordshire rectory a white-haired old man sits broken-hearted with his face to the wall . . .* Good luck to the archdeacon's daughter, I thought, who was plainly having no end of a time. It was only five minutes' walk to the Café Polska, and by 1.57 I was sitting at the table next to the window with a cup of coffee and a sandwich to make up for the lunch I'd missed talking to Sammy, and a packet of five Park Drive beside me, staring down Berwick Street like a tripper on the Brighton seafront with a *News Chronicle* under his arm looking for Mr Lobby Ludd. The Polska, by the way, was a real old Soho café, thick with the scent of Mitteleuropa and full of walrus-faced old boys reading foreign newspapers. In the old days you used to see White Russians there with high, Slav faces and spreading moustaches, all talking about their fathers' estates back in Nijinsky-Novgorod and looking as if they'd just stepped out of *A Sportsman's Sketchbook*, but it was sixteen years since the revolution now, and all the White Russians had gone.

Anyhow, five past two came, and then ten past, by which time I was getting so jumpy that I started playing a game I sometimes used to calm my nerves, which was to make up a football team composed of politicians. I'd just settled on George Lansbury as goalkeeper and was wondering whether Ramsay Mac and Arthur Ponsonby would do as fullbacks when I glanced out of the window and there she was, sauntering past the last of the market stalls, wearing one of those hats that are halfway between a cloche and a bluebell and a scarlet mackintosh that looked about three sizes too small. There was another girl with her, less well dressed and with a face that looked like a suet pudding, and as they came up level with the window she gave her a pat on the wrist and sent her off in the direction of Broadwick Street. A moment after that she breezed inside, stood in the doorway for a moment like a cat in a strange house, saw me at the table and gave a little nod.

'Sorry I'm late.'

'I've only just got here,' I said. 'Who's your friend?'

'Which friend?'

'The one you just said goodbye to.'

'Oh, she's not my friend.'

'Well, what is she then?'

'Oh, just somebody I see now and again.'

All this time I was shooting her little glances across the table, just to make sure I hadn't been fooling myself. But all the things I remembered were there. The blonde curls were mostly hidden by the hat, but the green eyes were sparkling away like nobody's business.

'Do you want a cup of tea?'

'No thanks. Here,' she said, 'I've brought your money.' She took a brown envelope out of her purse and plonked a handful of silver down on the tabletop. Six half-crowns and a couple of florins. One of the half-crowns went rattling onto the floor, so I bent down and picked it up.

'That's only nineteen shillings.'

'Is it?' She didn't seem particularly interested. 'Well, I'll give you the rest another time.'

She was still standing by the table, as if she couldn't make up her mind whether to sit down, but for some reason I've always been a sucker for girls who missed out on etiquette lessons at school, so I said: 'Funny our meeting like this.'

'Why's it funny?' She had a tiny birthmark just under her chin, I noticed, which made her look like the women you saw in the Gainsborough films.

'Well, me coming round to collect the rent and then lending you money instead.'

'I don't expect I'll stay there very long.'

'Why's that?' She was still standing by the table, but at least she'd put her bag down on the chair, which implied that she wouldn't go haring off again for a moment or two.

'I don't know. A girl likes a change. The woman in the flat below spent all last Sunday morning boiling a ham. I had to keep all the windows open half the day. I nearly went down and gave the old trout a piece of my mind.'

'Mrs Wisbeach?'

'That's the one.' She'd sat down now, and was making a great thing of snapping the metal fasteners on her bag open and shut, which made a terrific noise, like guncaps going off.

'She's invited me round there this evening,' I said.

'What for?'

So I explained about *Spirit Hands Have Touched Me* and the stuff about her husband joining the majority. Oddly enough, for the first time in our acquaintance she didn't look as if she was about to throw the cruet at me or turn me in to a policeman for making improper advances. Instead she said, quite fiercely: 'You ought to go.'

38

'Why's that?'

'My friend went to a seance once. She said her grandmother came and talked to her and said she shouldn't see her young man any more as he had designs. And after that she joined some funny religion where you had to dress up in a sheet and go off on charabanc rides to the Sussex Downs.'

'I tell you what,' I said. 'Seeing as you're so interested, why don't you come with me?'

'Come where?'

'To Mrs Wisbeach's.'

She looked a bit doubtful. 'Well, I suppose I might.'

'That's the spirit,' I said, a bit diffidently now. 'I'll come and knock on your door beforehand, shall I?'

'All right . . . Look,' she said, rather as if she were explaining something to a backward child, 'I've got to go now. I said I'd meet my friend outside Selfridges. Come round at eight. There's a chance I might not be there. If I'm not there go down to Mrs Wisbeach's and I'll be along when I get back. That's if the smell of the bloody ham has gone. Fair enough?'

'Absolutely.'

As I watched her stalk back across Berwick Street with the bag slamming against her calves like Tom Mix's saddle-pack, I thought about all the other women I'd sat in cafés with. There were quite a few of them: Netta, who used to throw condescending glances at the waitresses as they set down the tea; Mrs Bence-Jones, who liked expensive places where the staff wore black pinafores and lisle stockings and called you 'sir' and 'madam'; Richenda, who was CP and never allowed herself to be taken to a Lyons without giving you a

39

lecture on how you were exploiting the proletariat. There was a poster-board full of adverts on the wall behind me, and I browsed through them for a while, marvelling at the number of chaps who were trying to sell sofas for £5, or reckoned they had a sure-fire advance tip for next year's Cesarewitch, and wondered if they knew girls like Gladys and how they dealt with them.

It was about half past two by now, and given that I wasn't seeing Gladys until eight I figured that the most useful thing I could do was to take my evening suit out of hock from the pawnbroker's in Carlisle Street using the quid Sammy had subbed me.

I'd just done this, and was wandering back down Rathbone Street thinking that it didn't look too bad and I could probably repair the places where the moth had got at it with a darning needle, when something deuced odd happened. Perched on the stairs at Rathbone Place with his back to the door was a tall, thin bloke in a trilby hat with a walking stick under his arm. Something in the set of his shoulders—they were a bit like upturned champagne bottles—told me I'd seen him before and, sure enough, when he creaked round to face me I saw it was my uncle George.

Uncle George. He'd have to be in his early sixties now, with one of those long sorry-jester's faces with grooves in it like a shove ha'penny board. He was the Old Lady's younger brother, but the Old Lady couldn't stand him and he tended to turn up only at funerals and weddings. Just now he was supposed to be living at Ramsgate with his wife, whom no one else in the family had so much as set eyes on. As I came up the stairs with the suit hanging over my arm he blinked a bit suspiciously and then worked out who I was.

'Is that you, James?'

'Hello, Uncle George.'

The odd thing about Uncle George turning up on the doorstep wasn't his actual presence—I'd had him round once or twice in the past when I lived in Bayswater trying to cadge ten-bob notes—but one or two tiny changes in his get-up that only a close relative like me would have noticed. For a start, he had a packet of fags in his hand and was smoking one of them: the old Uncle George had only smoked other people's. But there was something else about him too. Either his suit was a shade better cut or the expression on his face a bit less hangdog. For the moment I couldn't quite work it out, but there was no getting away from it: something, or someone, had picked Uncle George up by the scruff of the neck and given him a shake.

'Elsie all right?' I asked as I tugged open the door.

'Grand,' he said, sounding like Stanley Holloway doing one of his monologues. 'Right as rain. Righter than rain. Nice little place we've got now. You ought to come down and see us. Drage's sofa. Good bit of garden. Elsie'd be delighted.'

Uncle George was supposed to have 'married beneath himself'. On the other hand, no one quite knew how far this descent had gone.

'Business good?'

'Known it better.' Last time I'd heard he had some kind of job selling space on one of the local newspapers. 'Lot of foreigners, you know, on the game these days.'

Another of Uncle George's defining characteristics was that he could never bring himself to say whatever it was he'd come to say straight out. He had to gear himself up a bit. The remarks he liked to throw out when he first saw you had no value in themselves. They were just stepping stones that would eventually bring you to the other side of the stream. And so he mooched around the room for a while, like an old duck draggling through refuse at the river's edge, picked up a copy of the *Blue Bugloss* and stared disbelievingly at it as if all the poems were in Mandarin, squinted at a picture of Carole Lombard I'd cut out of *Film Fun* like a Free Church elder coming across a What the Butler Saw machine on Stranraer pier, and said a bit peevishly: 'Hell and all trouble I had in finding you, I don't mind saying.'

'Sorry to hear that.'

'Your mother didn't know the address. In the end I had to ask the feller you work for.'

'Mr Samuelson?'

'Jewish chap, isn't he?'

'Shouldn't be surprised.'

I still couldn't work out what Uncle George was after. It could have been anything from an offer to join him in the painting and decorating trade in Ramsgate to taking shares in some new company he'd got wind of before it filed for bankruptcy. While I was thinking about this, I took another look at him to see if I could spot anything else that was different, the way you look at a place you go on holiday to every year in case there's another factory chimney looming over the horizon. There wasn't much to report, except that the brindled hair was possibly a touch less grey than the last time I'd seen him and there was a tiny silver badge on the lapel of his coat that looked like a bundle of sticks tied together.

'Cigarette?' Uncle George wondered. The packet was half full, too, which was unprecedented. 'Not much of a place you got here.'

'It's handy for work.'

'I'm not saying it isn't. Nothing like working over the shop. Or next door to it . . . How old are you now, James? Thirty-five, is it?'

'Nearly thirty-four.'

'Mm.' Uncle George was a great one for 'mms' and 'ahs' and other vocables you'd have trouble finding in the *Shorter Oxford*. 'Lowered morale. Seen it all over the place. Young chaps with good educations in dead-end jobs. Or no jobs at all. The leader's always talking about it.'

'I don't quite follow, Uncle George.'

After that, of course, I got the lot. How Uncle George was branch secretary of the Ramsgate BUF. How someone called Captain Annesley-Jones, who had a hotline to Mosley himself, had wrung his hand. How the country needed shaking up, and Sir Oswald and his boys were just the chaps to do it. He prosed on like this for a good five minutes, while I sat politely on the room's solitary chair and tried to remember whether the birthmark was on the right side of Gladys's chin or the left.

'What does Elsie think about it?'

'Elsie. She's all for it.'

'Will she'd be joining the women's section?' I'd seen pictures of them in the *Mail*, and they were tough babies by all accounts.

'She went on one of the nature rambles,' Uncle George said, a touch stiffly. 'Round Romney Marshes. But exercise don't agree with Elsie. Puts a strain on her heart. So we agreed it would be best not to.'

I couldn't get over the idea of Uncle George in black riding breeches and a dark pullover, or whatever it was they wore, marching up and down Ramsgate High Street, but clearly he was just nuts about it. After that the conversation drifted off a bit, and there was talk of Elsie's mother, who I gathered they'd got quartered on the premises, but finally Uncle George drew himself up to his full height—it was rather like an ancient grasshopper seeing if all its limbs were in working order—and said: 'You know, you ought to join us James. It ud be the making of you.'

'Why me especially?'

'Young chap like you that's served King and country. There's a lot of ex-army blokes like us, you'll find.'

Uncle George's military experience, I should say, consisted of six months as orderly clerk in the Middlesex Regiment's barracks at Stanmore, before he got invalided out with dropped arches.

'No thanks, Uncle George.'

'Why not?'

'Not my kind of thing.'

'That's the kind of attitude that'll see the Empire handed back to a lot of natives that couldn't govern themselves if you gave them lessons,' Uncle George said sententiously.

Anyway, he went off a bit after this—you could tell how offended he was by the fact that he didn't try to touch me for ten bob—and I sat down in the chair again. Uncle George as a Blackshirt! Who would have thought it? Each to their own, of course, but it was a bit like the Old Lady becoming

44

a Jehovah's Witness or Sammy asking if I felt like coming out on a Salvation Army rally next Sunday afternoon.

It was about half past three by now, and a really keen lad of the kind you read about in the business papers would have gone back to Lexington Street and collected some more rent. But what with Sammy, and Gladys, and Uncle George, I thought I'd earned a bit of rest that afternoon. In the end, when I'd gone out to post a poem I'd written to the *Adelphi*—it would come back, of course, but somehow that was less bad than not sending it at all—and then hiked up to Oxford Street to look in the windows of some of the knock-down shops, I found myself writing a letter to the Old Lady.

Darling Mums,

Hoping this finds you well and not inconvenienced by the weather. Life here is very busy. As I think I may have told you, I have taken up an opening in the property business. Not a very nice class of person, but the hours are civilized, and the premises are in the West End, which is a mercy. Did you see the Bystander *report on the Guinness's party? It sounded very jolly and I was only sorry that a prior engagement—Lord Fortescue, the insurance people, I'm sure you know of them— kept me from attending.*

Best love,
James

All this was complete nonsense, of course, but it

45

was the kind of thing the Old Lady liked to read. A bit after that I went to post it in the box at the corner of Rathbone Street. Oddly enough, the little trail of tarmac and bits of stone was still there leading up to the entrance of my digs. Even odder, I noticed when I went back to my room, was that it went all through the front door into the entrance hall and stopped outside the door of the room opposite.

4

VOICES IN THE DARK

The tarts in the square talk only to each other
They never seem keen to talk to me.
Stare at their lipsticks in Lew Levy's caff
Over twopenny cups of tea.

James Ross, Soho Eclogues

'But it's not the concealment that I don't like about Tom's poems. It's the *classicism*.'

'Is it now?'

'Naturally, no one minds a bit of austerity. My father was a Plymouth Brother. I think I know a thing or two about austerity. No, it's his attitude to the lyric I can't stand.'

'You mean he ought to be more like the Georgians? Flecker and Squire and so on?'

'Well, that would be going a bit far. Much too far. But I think he could . . . *unbend* a bit.'

'I'm sure you're right.'

'When all's said and done, there are times when a tree has to be a tree, don't you think, rather than the raw material for Jesse's staff?'

I'm no good at waiting for things to happen. By the time I'd got rid of Uncle George, been up to Oxford Street and written to the Old Lady, it was still only just past four o'clock, and the three-and-a-half hours that had to be endured before I could breeze out and meet Gladys gaped like a cavern's mouth. All comes of being such a nervous chap, you see, and not taking enough healthy exercise. But by five I was in such a state about the evening's entertainment that I reckoned I ought to step out for a breath of air. Which was why I'd found myself at the *Crucible*'s office in Fitzroy Square listening to Mortimer-Smith, its editor, explaining why he didn't like 'The Love Song of J. Alfred Prufrock'.

It was one of those brisk afternoons at the fag end of October, with the wind slamming in against the glass—the *Crucible* was on the third floor—and making the window frames quiver. Outside in the square the trees were bent back against the railings and the twilight was coming on, and there were chaps in mackintoshes with pork pie hats jammed down on their heads—used-car salesmen, I reckoned, on their way home from Warren Street—lighting fags underneath the street lamps.

'Between you and me, I stopped subscribing to the *Cri*,' Mortimer-Smith said. He was sitting with his chair tipped back and one foot resting on the table in front of him. 'Oh, it's a smart enough concern all right, but I just couldn't get used to it.'

'There's no accounting for taste.'

Do you know those literary magazines, I wonder? The *Crucible* had been going for a couple of years, and you sometimes saw copies of it in the snootier kind of bookshop. The original proprietor had been a bishop's son who'd run away from Eton, felt guilty about his inheritance and figured that he ought to make amends to the proletariat from whom it had been plundered. Then it had been bought by a Liberal peer who wanted to do his bit for culture. The articles about workers' solidarity and rallying round the banner had given way to pieces about André Breton and the Surrealist challenge, but

48

Mortimer-Smith didn't seem to mind. He had a good story about Lytton Strachey once tapping him for his cab fare home after a party. Anyhow, the *Crucible* came out monthly, or sometimes only six-weekly, paid ten bob for a poem and two quid for a story, and practically anything got printed in it if its author was prepared to buy Mortimer-Smith a double whisky in the Fitzroy Tavern just around the corner.

'Actually,' Mortimer-Smith said, 'I've got something you might be interested in.' He was a tall, thin chap of about forty, whose first book of poems had been praised for its 'considerable delicacy' by Siegfried Sassoon.

'What's that?'

'Well, Chalkie'—Chalkie was the *Crucible*'s proprietor—'thinks we ought to be expanding the mag. There's no money to do it, of course, but one of the things he thought we might run to is a dramatic critic. Highbrow stuff, of course. You'd have to go to those Workers' Theatre things in the East End, and write pieces about the drama of social realism and so on.'

'Noël Coward the prophet of decadence? Maugham as capitalist running dog? That kind of thing?'

'Well, not as *engagé* as that. I'm not sure where Chalkie stands politically these days. I did hear he'd been seen dining with Arthur Ponsonby. But I think he'd draw the line at capitalist running dogs.'

'How much will it pay?'

I've always believed that distinguished cultural services don't come cheap, you see.

'Let's see. You'd have to go to two or three pieces a month, I should think. And then there's

49

the travelling. I daresay we could manage three guineas. You've written on drama before, I take it?'

'Up to a point.'

No doubt about it I thought, as Mortimer-Smith showed me some press notices he'd been sent about a production shortly to be staged by the Hoxton Workers' Guild, where all the actors were supposed to represent the parts of an internal combustion engine, things were definitely looking up. What with the extra tin that Sammy was paying me and this bit of backsheesh from the *Crucible*, my income had just risen by about ten quid a month. Why, I might even be able to say goodbye to the digs in Rathbone Place and take a furnished flat or something up West. Plus there'd be money to spend on Gladys—if she'd let me spend it, that is.

Outside in the square the wind was still bending the trees back against the railings, but the men in the pork-pie hats had gone. There were some proof sheets lying on the desk next to Mortimer-Smith's foot, and I picked them up.

'What's in next month's?'

'There's that story of Alaric Littlejohn's we had trouble with. You know, the one where Cyril and Jacinth sit in silence by the water meadows listening to the nightingale. Then there are those translations from the Finnish. Oh, and Lady Laetitia Pilkington writing about why she's joined the BUF.'

I remembered Uncle George standing on the stairs at Rathbone Place. 'What does she say?'

'Oh, she says it does her old heart good to see some clean-living young men marching down the streets and not growing their hair long and sitting in cafés writing immoral poems.'

'I see.'

It was about six o'clock now. The first surge of people heading to the Tube or the buses in Oxford Street had stopped, and the darkness was welling up in the square.

'Do you want a drink?'

'I've got to go and see that chap Connolly at the Criterion bar. Chalkie wants him to write something for us. It's a shame. I wanted to ask you about John Drinkwater.'

Fact is, I wasn't too irked about Mortimer-Smith's previous engagement. He was a great one for knocking them back and then talking about his girl, who was called Mona and lived in Ealing with her parents and disapproved of the bohemian life he led. Considering some of the bohemians I've hung about with, I'd say she didn't know how lucky she was, but there you are.

Anyway, I was so bucked, what with the drama critic's job and the money that would soon be coming in, that I decided to go down to the Marquis of Granby and see if any of the old gang were about. But it was early days for the serious boozers and the place was full of art-student girls with berets on their heads and black display folders under their arms, so after I'd had a pint of mild-and-bitter, which tasted as if cockroaches had been crawling through the pipes, and smoked a couple of Abdullas, which I'd bought on the strength of my new job, I headed south and took a leisurely saunter along Oxford Street. Then, noting that the clock on the front of Bourne and Hollingsworth said ten to eight, I walked down into Dean Street.

Here a pile of old newspapers had spilled out over the road, there were two or three seedy-looking middle-aged blokes in overcoats stalking up

51

and down the pavement, obviously on the lookout for tarts, and a nancified youth with his collar and tie all over the place was being sick into the gutter: just an ordinary night in Soho, in fact. The lights were shining out of the windows of the restaurants, which were full of people having an early supper before they went of to the theatre, and as I strolled past I found myself staring at them. The women were mostly in evening gowns, and the blokes, if they weren't wearing dinner jackets, were togged out in the kind of suits you see on the dandified exquisites in the *Tatler* and the *Bystander*. I'm not an envious chap, you understand, but it made me wonder just how long I'd sat in any kind of restaurant with any kind of woman, let alone with the Hon. Miss Petunia Piprag breathing Chablis into my ear and murmuring that she'd heard Noël's new one—and how clever of you to get the tickets, darling—was simply divine.

And then, just as I came up level with the Toreador, which didn't open until 8.30 and still had the blinds pulled down over the long expanse of window that looked out onto the street, something deuced odd happened. Over on the other side of Dean Street there were two or three blokes hanging about near the doorway of the Cadenza—this was shut, too—and suddenly one of them came haring over the road, stopped dead like an athlete who's about to launch a javelin, took what looked like a half-brick out of his pocket and lobbed it through the Toreador's plate-glass. There was an almighty racket, like the time the Old Lady's Welsh dresser collapsed and half the tea service came to grief under it, and the bloke stood there for a second rubbing his hands together and then hared off back in the direction of Soho Square with the bits of glass crunching under his feet as he ran.

For a moment I wondered about going after him, but he was already twenty yards away by this time—he could have given Charlie Paddock a run for his money by the look of him. At the same time there was a little voice in my ear telling me to sling my hook sharpish. No doubt Sammy would have an idea why some little chap with a toothbrush moustache didn't like the set of his window. Sammy could have the broken glass swept up too. Plus it was nearly five to eight now, and I didn't want to be late for Gladys, who, despite her own performance earlier that afternoon, didn't strike me as the kind of girl who'd stand being kept waiting for more than thirty seconds. And so, casting a last look back in the direction of Soho Square, where the little chap with the toothbrush moustache was still going full pelt, I crossed over the road and lounged off in the direction of Meard Street.

As it turned out, I'd have been better off staying put at the Toreador and giving Sammy a hand with the brush and dustpan. Dead on eight I was halfway up the stairs at Number 3, paused just long enough to register the music coming out of the door of Sibierski's flat, and then banged on Gladys's door. What do you know? There was no answer. I hung around for a bit, on the off chance that she'd been getting out of the bath or feeding the cat, or doing any one of the half-dozen things women do when they've decided to string you along, but by ten past and another half-dozen despairing thumps on the door, I gave up and trudged downstairs to Mrs Wisbeach's on my own. There was an old chap in a bowler hat and a British Warm coming up the stairs

53

as I reached the door, but before either of us could ring the bell the door swung open and there on the mat stood Gladys.

'Oh hello,' she said, ignoring the chap in the bowler hat, who was gawping at her like Caesar when Cleopatra crawls out of the carpet. 'I thought I'd come down early. I hope you don't mind.'

'Not at all.'

'You'd better come in. The medium's here. I think Mrs Wisbeach wants to make a start.'

She was wearing an evening dress not unlike the ones I'd seen through the windows in Dean Street twenty minutes ago, and a pair of those black gloves that go all the way up to the elbow (a girl once told me that the real experts stop them from unravelling with a dab or two of spirit gum) and looked uncannily like the vamp in the kind of film where young Lord Sebastian, up from the varsity for the day, strays into one of those nightclubs his mother would have a fit about if only she knew. By this time I was in Mrs Wisbeach's front room, where there were about half a dozen people assembled in the region of the fireplace all looking horribly self-conscious and trying not to stare at the table, which had been covered with a black cloth and had the chairs pulled up to it very close.

'Why, Mr Ross,' Mrs Wisbeach said, breezing over from the fireplace. 'How good of you to come. And to invite Miss Marlborough too.'

Heaven knows how I'd been expecting Mrs Wisbeach to get herself up for the evening's events—I suppose I had a faint memory of Netta's mother in a sort of diamanté corset referred to as her 'bridge coat'—but this was a real eye-opener. She was wearing a kind of stiff black affair of what

54

could very well have been black bombazine, had her hair piled up under a toque that would have done credit to Edith Sitwell. There was a definite smell of crème de menthe, and also—presumably from the black bombazine—a terrific counter-reek of camphor.

'This is Mr Laal,' Mrs Wisbeach said, once we'd shaken hands, 'who will be conducting this evening's ceremonies,' and a little Indian chap, dressed western style but with white gaiters instead of trousers, came over from the mantelpiece and nervously bobbed his head.

'Mr Laal is a most accomplished voyager into the great unknown,' Mrs Wisbeach said, a bit too loudly for the room. 'We are extremely fortunate to have him preside over our little gathering.'

'I'm sure you're right.'

Mrs Wisbeach lowered her voice to a stage whisper. 'Between ourselves, some of my friends would prefer it if we did not have a coloured gentleman. But I tell them that seekers after the truth must, of all things, be broad-minded.'

By this time I'd had a chance to eye up the crowd over by the fireplace. There were a couple of middle-aged to elderly gents with brindled hair, an old girl with a blue-pattern version of what Mrs Wisbeach was wearing, and a younger woman with a chalk-white face who'd clearly never been instructed in the correct use of a lipstick standing to one side of them, with one arm resting on the mantelpiece and her marcelled hair gleaming back out of the mirror. Gladys looked as out of place as a hoopoe on a lawn full of starlings. I took another glance at her—all the seekers after truth were talking among themselves, which had clearly put her in a tremendous sulk—and decided, something I'd been fretting about as I came up Dean Street, that she really was my kind of girl. All my life, you see, I've been a sucker for those disdainful types who might just condescend to make a date for next Tuesday fortnight if it isn't the evening their Aunt Daphne's up in town for the knitting exhibition. I don't know why, but there it is.

'I think that as we are all assembled, we may begin,' Mrs Wisbeach announced, again in a voice that suggested someone ought to tape up the windows pretty quick, and there was a general movement towards the table. As I went I took a squint at Mr Laal, who'd been engaged in conversation by the old girl in the blue-pattern sack. He looked desperately anxious and his fingers were positively drumming against the sides of his trousers. Mrs Wisbeach, meanwhile, was directing people to their chairs.

'I think, Esmé, that you had better sit next to Mr Warburton. And Miss Marlborough, if you could possibly . . .'

Whatever hope I'd had of sitting next to Gladys vanished on the instant, as Mrs Wisbeach squeezed her in between one of the old gents with brindled hair and Mr Laal himself. I ended up between the second old gent and the girl with the butcher's block lips. There was one of those old-fashioned kerosene lanterns in the centre of the table and this, having first had someone switch off the electric light, Mrs Wisbeach dimmed down to about half its strength. I'd worked out by now that my initial assessment of Mrs Wisbeach was bang right, and that she was as tough an old girl as they come; the Old Lady would probably have fallen on her shoulder like a lost sister. This point was proved a moment or two later when Mr Warburton, the elder of the two middle-aged to elderly gents, asked if he could have a glass of water and was told he'd have to wait.

'Why not put out the cards, Bertha?' the younger of the middle-aged to elderly gents diffidently proposed. 'That's if you're in the mood, of course.'

Mrs Wisbeach thought about this. There was a faintly irritated look on her face. The smell of the camphor seemed stronger than ever. 'It does not do to question the cards too often,' she said. 'Besides, we have a greater object in view.'

I took a look at Gladys and saw that she was just drinking it in, mouth half open, like a goldfish.

'In fact, I had thought . . . But no.' And here Mrs Wisbeach gave a kind of artificial laugh that would have done credit to the juvenile lead in a musical comedy, and had a whispered conversation with Mr Laal. Whatever she said clearly flummoxed him, as he folded his hands across his chest and looked dead sulky.

'As Mr Laal wishes for a further period of time in which to ready himself,' Mrs Wisbeach announced, 'I had thought we might begin with planchette. Mr Laal says that he is not prepared to be associated with this undertaking. Of course, I respect this. And yet the quest for truth takes us to many doors, some open, some closed. If Mr Laal will excuse us, I confess that I am not averse to this experiment.'

Well I wasn't either, if it was going to keep Gladys happy. Anyhow, there was a minute or so's discussion, during which Mr Warburton prosed on grimly about 'unwise influences' and 'evil

57

communications', under Mrs Wisbeach's gimlet eye, after which she disappeared to a room at the back—a fusillade of yaps from Hercules, who'd clearly been locked up in there—and returned with a little heart-shaped wooden board with a couple of casters beneath it and a pencil stub jammed in the end. Now, I'd never seen a planchette in action before, but Corporal Hackett, with whom I used to sit steaming open the mail in the hut on the South Downs, used to swear by it and reckoned he'd won the Derby three years running on the strength of the hints it had dropped.

'You are sure, Mr Laal, that you would not care to act as our guide?' Mrs Wisbeach asked. But Mr Laal shook his head.

He said very loudly: 'It is a childish thing.'

'But you yourself, Mr Laal, have told me on more than one occasion that to reach the spirit world unorthodox methods may sometimes be needed.'

'No good will come of it.'

There was a sheet or two of cartridge paper lying on an occasional table a few feet away—the top-most one had a shopping list written on it, I noticed—and Mrs Wisbeach spread one out carefully on the table.

'This is *too* exciting,' Gladys said.

'It is very uncertain that anything will happen,' Mrs Wisbeach said, a bit like a schoolmistress who's promised the Lower Fourth the afternoon off to play Lax and then changed her mind five minutes later.

The trick with spirit-writing on a planchette board—I'd had full details from Corporal Hackett—is that you do it in pairs, with each person

58

pressing one hand on the board. This reduces the chances of anyone cheating, though as you're writing upside down I can't see how anyone could if they wanted to. Anyhow, the other old chap, whose named was Atterbury, and the girl with the lipstick had first go, and a fine old mess they made of it. At one point the board slid off over the edge of the table and fell into Mr Laal's lap. Then it went round in a circle, and there was some doubt as to whether it had produced the word 'Uttoxeter'. I had a turn, assisted by Mrs Wisbeach, whose grip on the board was surprisingly firm, and got nowhere. Finally, it was Gladys and Mr Warburton's turn, who cheered up no end when he realized he got to hold Gladys's hand into the bargain.

And then something odd happened. At first the board wobbled a bit. Then it shot off across the table and nearly collided with old Atterbury's elbow. After another thirty seconds, though, it settled into a regular up-and-down motion, inching forward over the paper. A trail of script, done in small shaky letters but more or less intelligible, began to flow out of the underside.

Borne on the black tide

'What does it mean?' Gladys asked.

'Shakespeare, isn't it?' Mr Atterbury suggested. 'That line in *Macbeth*?'

I took a look round the table. Gladys had put her knuckles up to her mouth. Mr Warburton was looking a bit mystified, but not at all unhappy at the sensation he'd caused. Mrs Wisbeach had a sort of exalted expression on her face, like a priestess turning over the entrails. Only Mr Laal looked cross.

'We must ask it who it is,' Mr Atterbury said. He

59

sounded as if he was ready to have a heart attack on the spot. 'Who are you?'

But the board was already marching away again. Only Hercules's yapping broke the silence. Mrs Wisbeach craned over the table, trying to make out the words.

The door will be shut

'Which door?' Mr Warburton demanded. He clearly hadn't had so much fun since Armistice Night. 'And who'll shut it, I wonder?'

There was another furious up-and-down movement, so violent that Gladys gave a little shriek and the board sailed away again in the direction of Mr Atterbury's midriff.

The gaoler has his price

'It's definitely a quotation,' Mr Warburton said. 'Have you got a *Chambers* by any chance, Bertha?'

'This is too exciting,' Gladys said again. Mr Laal made a contemptuous noise under his breath.

The board was running out of steam. It made one more crawling motion over the cartridge paper and then stopped dead. Mrs Wisbeach traced the line with her finger.

Follow her always

'Well, I must say I don't understand this at all, Bertha,' Mr Atterbury said. 'Hang on, what's it doing now? Oh, I see.'

Mr Laal gave a little giggle.

'An occupational hazard, I'm afraid,' Mrs Wisbeach said.

I'd last seen the word earlier that afternoon chalked on the wall of the Broadwick Street urinals, but there you are.

Mrs Wisbeach picked up the sheets of cartridge paper and inspected them a bit grimly, as if she suspected them of harbouring other obscenities she hadn't yet spotted, rolled them into a cylinder and stowed them away in a drawer. The planchette was put in a cardboard box. 'I think we had better have some refreshment,' she said, 'and then recommence, or Mr Laal will never forgive us for bringing him all this way.'

She made it sound as if Mr Laal had been flown in from Delhi on the Empire Mail, whereas I could see the return half of a bus ticket sticking out of his jacket pocket.

Afterwards there was some extremely pale sherry and a plate of drop scones that Mrs Wisbeach produced from the kitchen, but somehow all the fun had gone out of the evening. I tried to get Gladys to one side while the bunfight was going on, but she was in a huddle with Mr Warburton, telling him about the time a gypsy had told her fortune at Blackheath Fair. The thought that the main event had already packed up and gone home had pretty obviously occurred to Mr Laal, as once he'd put away his second glass of sherry he rapped the glass smartly on the sideboard and said: 'Ladies and gentlemen . . . I must positively *insist*.'

I wondered how much he stood to make from the evening. A chap once told me that mediums made a fortune, but Mr Laal didn't look as if he'd known a square meal since the National Government got in. We went back to our seats at the table and Mrs Wisbeach turned the kerosene lamp down to its lowest notch. Then she said: 'Who is to be our guide into these realms of the unknown?'

'Best not to say a name,' Mr Warburton volunteered. 'They can sometimes turn nasty, you know.'

'Hush,' Mrs Wisbeach said, making a gesture with her hand.

Whatever else you might say about Mr Laal, he was clearly determined to give value for money. First he went into a kind of trance—you could still hear Hercules yapping away in the background—quite motionless, except for the tips of his fingers which drummed a bit on the tablecloth. Then he started making little hissing noises. All this, needless to say, we attended to with the gravest consideration. About five minutes went by, and then Mr Atterbury said: 'Would it help if we made some entreaty?'

'Be silent, Edwin,' Mrs Wisbeach countered.

'Is he going to say anything?' Gladys asked.

I could hear Mrs Wisbeach drawing in her breath to tick her off, when all of a sudden Mr Laal began to speak—not in the exaggerated sing-song he'd used when bidding us to the table, but in a high-pitched little girl's voice that, when you came to think about it, wasn't at all unlike Shirley Temple's in *The Red-Haired Alibi*. I couldn't make head or tail of it. On the other hand, the effect on Mr Atterbury was electrifying.

'It's Edie. I know it is.'

'Hush, Edwin,' Mrs Wisbeach said.

'Edie that was taken from us before her time . . .'

The voice was going nineteen to the dozen now, still very high-pitched.

'Something about a rose garden in Godalming,' Mrs Wisbeach said, who'd been listening attentively, 'and the lamp-lighter treading his nightly round.'

'Edie never went out of Kent in her life . . .'

'And coming down the big dipper at Folkestone

62

fair.'

'If there was one thing Edie was afraid of it was heights . . .'

All of a sudden there was a terrific bang, as if someone's foot had swung against a table leg, and a crashing noise as a chair went over. Gladys gave a shriek. What with all the confusion it was a moment or two before anyone turned the electric light on. When they'd done this, Mr Laal was found sitting on the floor with a slightly dazed expression on his face and a hank of butter muslin half way out of his trouser pocket. I've always been led to believe that butter muslin is what they make ectoplasm out of, by the by.

Anyhow, there was a hell of a row, with people shouting and chairs rolling about, and Mrs Wisbeach, as far as I could make out, accusing Mr Warburton of putting the butter muslin there on purpose. Time to make a move, I thought to myself. The same idea had clearly occurred to Gladys, and the pair of us found ourselves outside Mrs Wisbeach's door about thirty seconds later. She looked a bit pale, I thought, and fantastically sulky.

'Well, that was a bit of a fiasco,' I said.

'Yes, wasn't it?' She had one foot on the staircase.

'It's only nine-fifteen. Shall we go and have a drink?'

'I can't tonight.'

'Why's that?'

'I've got a terrible headache. It's just come on.'

'Has it?'

'Yes.'

'I see.'

'The only thing to do is go back to my room and

lie down. You understand that, don't you?'

'Of course.' From back inside Mrs Wisbeach's flat there was a crescendo of yelps, which suggested that Hercules had joined the party. 'Some other time, then. For the drink, I mean.'

'I expect so,' she said, a shade listlessly. 'Goodnight.'

'Goodnight.'

I waited until I heard the door slam and then trudged down the staircase into the street, where there was fine drizzle falling and someone had left a pair of braces, of all things, hanging round the nearest lamp post. I'm a trusting sort of a chap, you see, and I had no idea whether the headache was genuine or whether she'd decided she just couldn't stand the sight of me. For a moment I thought about the other excuses I'd been served up with during the years. With Netta it had been rearranging her photo album. Mrs Bence-Jones had a line about getting her accounts in order. But there was no point crying over spilt milk, so I hunched my shoulders up under my coat against the drizzle—it was coming down pretty hard now—and mooched off down the south end of Dean Street, past the novelty shop and the Jewish tailor's and the place that sold Yank mags, thinking I'd go and have a drink in one of the pubs in Shaftesbury Avenue.

I'd just stopped to look at one of the ads in a newsagent's window—you know, the one where young ladies with chests for sale invite gentlemen callers—when I heard the sound of a pair of high heels, going very fast, coming up on the other side of the pavement. God knows what instinct told me to do it, but for some reason I turned into the newsagent's doorway next to one of those ads for the *Daily Mail* that promise a pair of silk stockings to anyone who takes out a subscription, and nearly trod on a French letter that someone had left there. Then, looking up, I discovered the hunch I'd had was bang right. It was Gladys, haring off in the direction of Old Compton Street as fast as her legs could carry her.

A gentleman, in these circumstances, would have allowed a discreet interval to pass and then gone off the other way. But I'm not a gentleman. Plus, I was kicking myself for having fallen for the headache routine. Anyway, keeping close to the shopfronts, with my chin well down into my mackintosh, I decided to see where she was off to. There were one or two people about, and a whole crowd of drunks spilling out of a club on the corner, but I managed to keep her in my sights as she turned into Old Compton Street. Can't be going far, I thought, not in those heels, and, sure enough, after another thirty yards or so she stopped outside a pub doorway, where a little chap who'd clearly been waiting for her stepped out of the shadows, fastened onto her arm and steered her inside. And what do you know? It was the bloke with the slicked back hair and the toothbrush moustache who'd chucked the half-brick through the Toreador's front window an hour and a half before.

5

WEST END CENTRAL

On the wall of the male urinal
Clear for all to see:
'Detective Smith knows how to gee,
Tell him he's a —— from me.'

James Ross, Soho Eclogues

'I was standing by the banquette when it happened,'
Mr Samuelson said. 'Gave me the hell of a shock, I
don't mind telling you.'

'That's right.'

'And then half the glass went into the carpet
under the window. I had to ask Daphne to get it out
with a toothpick.'

'That must have been tricky.'

'But that's not all,' Mr Samuelson said. The
smoke from his cigar kept dribbling into the
corner of his right eye and making it water. 'Next
morning, when I came down to unlock, someone'd
painted "Yid" all over the front door. Now, why
would anyone want to do a thing like that? I'm an
Ulsterman myself, but it gave me no end of a turn.'

Mr Samuelson quite often said he was an
Ulsterman.

'There are some funny people about these days,'
I said.

'You can say that again.'

It was two evenings later and we were standing
in the vestibule of the Toreador looking out into

Dean Street. Outside the Cadenza some men were unloading a piano from a horse and cart, and a couple of tarts with faces like death's heads were having a row under the street lamp.

'Do you know,' Mr Samuelson said, 'there are times when I could give all this up?'

'It's the fashionable thing to do,' I said. 'The newspapers are full of stockbrokers swapping the hurly-burly of their London lives for fruit farms in the West Country.'

'So they are. I've often thought about it. But then Beryl'—Beryl was his wife—'always says, "What would you do if you didn't have the Toreador to go to?" and you wouldn't credit it, but I'm blowed if I know.' A little old man in a dinner jacket that looked as if Metternich had had it made up for him to attend the Congress of Vienna wandered through the door and Mr Samuelson stared at him hopefully. 'Anyway, I'll be in my office if you want me.' He shuffled off in the direction of the staircase, leaving me with Edgar the doorman, Elvira, the cloakroom girl who helped people with their coats, and the little dinner-jacketed old man.

As for the geography of the Toreador, the hallway, where I was lurking in my evening suit and a pair of outsize black Oxfords I'd borrowed from one of the waiters, led off to the supper room and a couple of hidey-holes where you could play cards. If you ordered a drink after eleven you were given a saucerful of antique sausage meat to keep up the pretence that you were dining late. The police came by about once a month and were generally given a bottle of whisky. Occasionally they were allowed to stage a raid, which Sammy said was good for publicity. My job, as itemized by Sammy, was to give Edgar a hand on the door when the place got crowded, make sure nobody nicked anything or went upstairs to the private rooms or got too free with any of the girls, make sure there was a room spare for the singers to change in, bring the band drinks when they wanted them, and if anything really serious happened let the alarm off and run onto the dance floor shouting, 'Fire!' in a very loud voice while at the same time remembering to call the men 'sir' and the ladies 'madam'.

'Excuse me,' the little old man said, a bit confidingly. He'd taken off his coat and scarf and given them to Elvira. 'Does a young lady called Geraldine work here?'

'No one of that name on the staff, sir.'

'Are you sure?'

'Positive, sir.'

He rambled off in the direction of the supper room. Elvira and I exchanged glances.

Most people assume that nightclubs are dens of vice and debauchery, with cocaine fiends hiding in the wainscoting and white slavers ready to pounce on unprotected vicars' daughters who've wandered in there in mistake for the local bridge club. In fact, the Toreador was about as debauched as a glee-singing competition in Hampstead Garden Suburb. There was a rule that the girls weren't allowed to get off with anybody, but Sammy didn't mind as long as it was done discreetly. A proper tart who tried to get through the door would be chucked out into Dean Street by Edgar before you could say 'Mrs Meyrick'. The real trouble among the clientele, I always found, was with middle-aged women who'd decided their lives had been wasted and it was time to let themselves go.

68

But there weren't any of those here tonight. Thursday was always a quiet evening at the Toreador, and after I'd nipped upstairs and checked the landing—there was nothing doing except the light burning under Sammy's door—brought Elvira a dandelion and burdock from the bar and made sure a chap in one of the card rooms who'd ordered a magnum of champagne all to himself and was guzzling it like a drunken sailor hadn't passed out, there wasn't a great deal to do. So I shot my cuffs, in that classy way Jack Buchanan does on the films, and stood in the vestibule smoking a cigarette and saying 'Good evening, sir' and 'Chilly for the time of the year, madam' as folk came in through the door. There was a minor flap when somebody said that Lady Furness was in the club, but I'd seen Lady F.'s picture in the *Sketch* the other week playing ten-pin bowling with the Prince, and this one definitely wasn't her. And then all of a sudden a blonde piece in an evening gown who'd gone blinking short-sightedly past a couple of times turned out to be an old friend of mine called Marjorie.

'You're looking very smart, James,' she said. 'What are you doing here?'

I explained about collecting Sammy's rents in Meard Street. Then something struck me and I said: 'Whatever happened to my friend Hastings?'

'Who?'

'The chap I introduced you to that time at the Pegasus Club.' She was still looking a bit mystified. 'The one I worked for selling carpet-cleaning lotion who said he'd nearly become a vicar.'

'Oh, you mean Claude. I don't know. It didn't last very long.'

'No?'

'He was very possessive. Didn't even like it if the bus conductor winked at you. I said to him: "A girl's got to look out for herself, you know. We're not living in the Victorian age."'

'I expect he went back to his wife.'

'I expect he did.'

Marjorie was a nice girl, but she ate men for breakfast. Just then a chap who looked exactly liked Lloyd George, apart from a rather glazed expression on his face, came stumbling through the door and she went bouncing off to greet him. Anyway, coming across Marjorie like this reminded me of all the trouble I'd been in when I last saw her, and pretty soon I was brooding away about Gladys, who I hadn't seen since the hoedown at Mrs Wisbeach's. Fact is, I'd been round there a couple of times on the pretext of some repairs Sammy wanted to do, but no one had answered the door and I didn't fancy leaving a note. Meanwhile there were people coming into the club in dribs and drabs: a couple of MPs, who knew Sammy from somewhere; a gaggle of young sparks I'd have said had just been watching the boat race if it hadn't been October; one or two rich-looking Jewish blokes with fingers like saveloys and women in fox furs simpering on their arms. Just as I was wondering if I oughtn't to go to the aid of an old girl who'd got the hem of her dress stuck fast in the door, Edgar sloped across and said: 'I don't like the look of that lot.'

I took a squint in the direction he was nodding at and decided I didn't like the look of them either. Three biggish chaps of about my age, or something under it, all looking as if they'd just come back from an afternoon spent playing for the London Irish at Richmond Park. The giveaway, though, was that they were clearly sizing the place up, staring at the waiters through the open door of the supper room and then reckoning up the distance back to where Edgar and I were planted outside. Trouble for someone, I thought, but then a message came through from the cashier that the float was running low and I had to trek down to the safe in the bowels of the building—this was another of my jobs—and ferry up another sack of half-crowns and florins.

After that I was summoned to deal with a rat that was making its presence felt in the kitchen—there were some clubs where the vermin man wouldn't go into the basement without a loaded revolver—and find Elvira a safety pin for her dress, which was coming away at the back—it's a glamorous old life, you see, working in a nightclub—and it was a good half-hour before I got back to the entrance hall. There was no one much about, although it looked suspiciously as if someone had been sick into one of the aspidistras, and Edgar was parked outside in the street smoking a fag. There were flakes of ash over the lapels of his dinner jacket, and he looked uncannily like the butler in one of those Ibsen plays who's just about to mooch in and announce that the master has hanged himself in the shrubbery.

'Everything all right?'

'Nothing you could complain of.'

'That new girl they had singing "The Little Things You Do" didn't sound too bad.'

'That's your opinion,' Edgar said. He was one of those lugubrious types, who wouldn't have smiled at a thousand a year raise. 'I keep telling

His Lordship we ought to have that Dorina who sings with Heywood and Hay—I saw them last week at the Finsbury Empire with Rosalind Wade's Radiolympia girls—but catch him listening to me. Ho no.'

He was just on the point of offering me a fag when there was a terrific thumping noise back inside the Toreador and the London Irish front row appeared on the doorstep. They had Marjorie with them, and as I looked on the one nearest to me turned and said something to her.

'Cheek!' Marjorie said.

Before I knew what I was doing I was squeezed into the space between them, close enough to see that the chap was a good three inches taller than me and at least a stone heavier. To make matters worse he had brilliantined hair and one of those 'You be d——d' expressions on his face.

'Is there a difficulty, sir?'

'F—— off.'

'I don't think there's any need for language like that, sir.' Christ knows what help this would be, but it was something Sammy reckoned we ought to say on these occasions.

At this point one of the others joined in. The curious thing was that he looked exactly like Corporal Hackett, whom I'd steamed open the envelopes with in the hut on the South Downs, and who'd died of Spanish Flu, poor b——r, on Armistice Night.

'F—— off.' Then, for good measure, he added, 'Kike.'

Now if there's one thing us Rosses are proud of it's our sturdy Highland ancestry. Next thing I knew there was a fist or two sailing through the air, and a proper roughhouse involving the four of us, Edgar, who'd prudently armed himself with a dustbin lid, and Marjorie, who tried to hit the chap who'd cheeked her with her handbag but only succeeded in fetching me a terrific clout on the ear. Then a whistle went off somewhere, there was a noise of feet running towards us, someone kicked my legs away from underneath me and, by the time I could make out what was happening again, I was sitting in the gutter on top of some cauliflower stalks someone had dumped there with a policeman shining a torch into my face and demanding what the b——g hell I was doing.

In my experience you need tact and diplomacy to get out of these situations, so I said, 'I was merely going to the aid of one of my colleagues, officer. The young lady over there.'

'When I come by, you'd just hit that gentleman bang on the jaw.'

Two of the London Irish front row seemed to have disappeared, but the one who'd called me a kike was having an animated conversation with a second policeman. Marjorie and Edgar had vanished. With any luck they'd gone back into the club to fetch Sammy.

'Too f——g right I did.' Perhaps it wasn't a time for tact and diplomacy.

'Unprovoked assault, he says. Can't say I don't agree with him.'

Anyway, next thing I knew I was in the back of a police van barrelling down Dean Street as if the Revolution had broken out at the other end of it, with the barred windows breaking up the light from the street lamps like a row of daggers. Fact is, what with the thump on the ear and having gone down

73

on the tarmac like a sack of prime King Edward's, I wasn't feeling too sharp. I had a feeling, too, that there was something odd going on, which is to say that the blokes had been looking for trouble and didn't much care where they found it. But why should they pick on the Toreador? What was the deal with Marjorie? And why should they pick on me? Anyhow, a couple of minutes later the driver slid round the corner of Oxford Street into the Tottenham Court Road like someone practising for the TT races and we stopped outside West End Central.

As for being arrested, the curious thing is that you notice tiny details. By rights when they marched me up to the duty sergeant I should have been loudly protesting my innocence and trying to remember Tommy Kilmarnock's telephone number. When it came to it, though, I found I was registering the fact that the desk sergeant had a cold sore starting on his upper lip and whoever'd been doing the *Mirror* crossword that lay on the desk hadn't yet managed 13 across. Plus someone hadn't swept the floor that morning and there was a Weights packet stamped flat into the tiles.

From the look the desk sergeant gave me you'd have thought I was Monday's fish being served up at the Lord Mayor's banquet.

'What's he done then?'

While they were explaining, and the desk sergeant was writing it down in his book, I had a look round the vestibule. There was no one much about, except a very old lady who seemed to have gone to sleep on one of the benches and a little Asiatic chap with no shoes on. Finally the desk sergeant signed his initials at the bottom of the

74

report—he did this with a kind of infinite disgust—slammed the ledger shut, caught my eye and said: 'Anything you want to say?'

I put on my toniest voice, the one that had got me the job in the accountancy firm at Hove, and announced to a point two or three feet above his head, 'I should like to telephone my lawyer, Mr Kilmarnock.'

'Fat chance of 'im coming out at this time of night.' It was about ten o'clock. 'It'll have to wait until morning.' He nodded at the constable who'd explained about the fight. 'You'd better put this man in number three.'

Number three was halfway along a corridor lit by a single electric light. As we came up to it the copper said: 'Better take your shoes off, chum.'

'Why's that?'

'Had a bloke in here last week tried to hang himself with the laces. Wallet?'

'Left it at home.' I took the shoes off and handed them over.

'Want a receipt?'

'No thanks.'

The cell was so tiny it could have been Princess Elizabeth's dolls' house. There was a bench running along the far wall and a chamber pot that stank to high heaven. On the wall someone had written *When apples are ripe, they're ready for plucking. Girls of sixteen are ready for . . .*, which I'd heard Max Miller say at the Stratford Empire a good two years ago. A little chap with a Charlie Chaplin moustache and the palest face you ever saw outside a vampire movie was sitting on the bench, so when the copper had finished locking up the door I said: 'What are you in for then?'

'Me?' he said, shyly. 'I've been done for follerin' Edna again.'

'Who's Edna?'

'Edna Allardyce.' There was a definite pride about the way he said this, like a bloke who's just won the best municipal allotment prize. 'The actress. I go and stand outside her flat and wave at her when she draws the blinds down.'

'What do you want to do that for?'

I'd seen a couple of films with Edna Allardyce in, but she wasn't really my type.

'I don't know. I just do. Another time I follered her into Selfridges when she was buying a nightdress.'

'Don't you get tired of it? Being had up, I mean?'

'No I don't. What are you in for?'

He was a friendly chap, so I explained about being lifted out of the gutter in Dean Street and he reckoned it sounded odd. 'Collusion,' he said. 'Put-up job. Shouldn't wonder if the police were waiting outside.'

'Why would they want to do that?'

'I don't know. These things are funny. I'd never have been arrested for follerin' Edna if her young man hadn't have liked it.'

He went quiet after this non sequitur, and after I'd looked round the cell again I settled down to think things through a bit. There was no light except for the bulb in the corridor, which threw giant shadows over the wall of the cell. It was pretty quiet, although once there was a terrific noise from further down the row which sounded like someone parting company with a sack of melons. In the distance you could hear footsteps moving about.

'What time will they let us out, do you think?'

But the little chap had gone to sleep, head back against the wall so you could see the glint of the fillings in his teeth. I decided I'd attempt to occupy myself by trying to recall the names of all the clubs in the Football League. I'd got as far as Notts County when there was a rap on the door of the cell and a voice said: 'Either of you blokes called Ross?'

'That's me.'

'You're wanted then.'

'Why's that?' He'd tugged open the door by now. The corridor looked the same, except for a huge pool of sick at the far end.

'B——g drunks,' the copper said, looking at the sick. 'I'd make them clean it up theirselves if it was down to me. Chap wants to see you.'

I looked at my watch. It was about midnight, which is a deuced odd time to be hoicked out of a police cell, I can tell you. 'Who's the chap?'

'Find out soon enough.'

He marched me off down the corridor and on through a warren of passageways and store cupboards until we got to a largish room with a couple of metal desks and a notice on the wall warning about the importation of seedlings liable to cause potato blight. Behind the second one a chap in a brown suit with parchment skin stretched tight over his face was reading the previous day's *News Chronicle*. When he saw me he waved away the copper who'd fetched me, put down the paper and said: 'Your name Ross?'

'That's me,' I said again.

'Saw your monicker on the charge sheet just now. Reckoned it might be you. Remember me?'

Fact is, it was the eyes that jogged my memory. Darting around like fish in a tank but completely expressionless. No doubt about them. It was Mr Haversham, who'd made himself dead unpleasant a couple of years ago and sent me on a wild-goose chase down to Sussex into the bargain. There was a bit of a silence while Haversham lit a fag and looked me up and down. I was still wearing my evening suit, of course, though my tie had come off during the scrap.

'What are you doing dressed up like a pox-doctor's clerk?' he demanded.

'It's my job.'

Haversham pulled on the cig two or three times. You could tell what a fag-merchant he was from the fact that he didn't even blink when the smoke drifted up into his face.

'Going up in the world, I see,' he said. 'What you in for then?'

So I explained about working for Sammy and the punch-up in Dean Street and coming to in the gutter with the copper shining a torch in my face.

'Hmm. Don't look too good,' Haversham said. He was staring at a sheet of paper that had appeared on the desk under the *News Chronicle*. 'Specially not with Mr Pendragon on the bench tomorrow. Regular down he's got against brawling in the street. You could be looking at fourteen days here.'

'It was a put-up job,' I told him. 'These blokes were looking for trouble. Ask anyone who was there and they'll tell you the same.'

'Bad business,' Haversham said, stretching out the words. 'Ve-ry bad business.' He looked pleased about something, like a cat that's strolled out into the garden at the precise moment the wind lifts a nest full of fledglings out of the tree above its head.

'Still, there's all sorts of ways you can get the charge dropped, you know.' He had another fag on by now, and the smoke was dribbling out of the corner of his mouth. 'All depends on you.'

'How does it depend on me?'

'Well, let's say you offer to help us with our enquiries.'

I'd helped Haversham with his enquiries before, and a fine old mess I'd been landed in. 'What enquiries would they be then?'

'All right.' There was a rickety old chair to one side of the desk and Haversham motioned me to sit on it. 'Let's have a talk. Just the two of us. Off the record. Like them other talks we used to have. You with me?'

'I suppose so.'

'That's the spirit.' The cigarette was half smoked down now. Somewhere above us there was a rumble of moving feet and what sounded like a table being turned over. 'There's some funny things going on in Soho just at the moment.'

'Nothing new about that. The Society for the Suppression of Vice's been campaigning here since 1847.'

'No, not that kind of thing. Other stuff. Bricks going through winders. Rubber shops getting smashed up and robbed. Isn't the usual mob, neither.'

'Which mob is it then?'

'Never you mind. Let's just say, nine times out of ten when that kind of thing happens I can make a fair guess at who's responsible. If it's not Jack Spot and his boys it's that Eyetie lot in Brewer Street. See what I mean? Now, you know anything about these Blackshirts?'

'Mosley's lot?'

'That's them. Lot of kids that'd be better off in the Boy Scouts if you want my opinion, but that's by the way. Anyhow, my information is that they're the parties we're after.'

'Why would the Blackshirts be turning over rubber shops in Soho?'

'Well, I've a notion. One thing is it's easy money. Second thing, blokes that own them shops aren't the kind that want the likes of me on their doorstep. Much sooner keep the thing quiet. Third thing, blow for decency and so on.'

I thought about Uncle George. He didn't seem like the kind of chap who'd want to spend his time throwing bricks through the windows of rubber shops, or even wanting to strike blows for decency, but you should never underestimate the puritanism of the British bourgeoisie. Mrs Bence-Jones's husband had been on the watch committee, shining torches at the courting couples in the cinema back row.

'What's all this got to do with me?'

'Well now. You taken a walk down the King's Road lately?'

'Not that I can remember.'

'Well, there's an old training college down there, which they've bought up and turned into a headquarters. The "Black House" I b'lieve they're calling it now. Plus there's a big recruiting drive going on, or so I hear.'

By this time the penny had dropped. 'You want me to join the BUF?'

'That's the ticket.'

'What if I don't want to?'

Haversham's eyes gleamed. 'Last Monday

morning,' he said, 'when Mr Pendragon was sitting on the bench, he gave a chap fourteen days just for waving his fist at another chap for blocking 'is shop doorway with a barrow-end. "Threatening behaviour". Just think what he'd do to you for punching a chap in the mug in Dean Street in plain view of two police officers.'

He had me over a barrel. Still, I thought, if a hopeless specimen like Uncle George could wangle his way into the BUF they'd surely welcome me with open arms.

'What do I have to do?'

'That's the spirit,' Haversham said. His eyes had that mad gleam in them that I remembered from last time. 'Hang around the King's Road and see what's going on. Keep your ears open, and if anyone mentions Soho report back to me.'

'I've got a job to do, you know.'

'Go down the King's Road in the evenings. That's when the place starts to fill up.'

'Those are my b——y hours,' I said. 'If I hadn't been working at the Toreador, I shouldn't be here now.'

'All right, all right,' Haversham said. His eyes had settled back in his head now, and I could see he was losing interest in me. He probably had someone else he wanted to blackmail in the next cell. 'Go on your evening off. Weekends, whatever.'

'How long do I have to do it for?'

Haversham lit another cigarette. The rasp of the match when he struck it on the wall echoed through the room, like someone marching over sandpaper. 'You find something that's worth my while hearing and we'll see,' he said. 'Holgate!'

The copper who'd brought me there, and had

clearly been hovering in the passage in case I started causing trouble, jumped back into the room like a jack-in-the-box.

'Give this bloke his duds, will you?'

And that was that. The copper took me back to the front entrance—the old lady and the Asiatic bloke had gone, but there was a chap in evening dress sitting on the bench with his head in his hands and a woman in a fur coat protesting that she was the Marchioness of Abergeldie and her solicitor would be round directly—somebody handed me a box containing my shoes and, five minutes later, I was out in the Tottenham Court Road wondering just exactly what I'd let myself in for. It was about a quarter to one and the rain was coming down like billy-oh, but what with the events of the past couple of hours that was the least of my worries. They could have been canoeing down Oxford Street for all I cared. And so I hunched the shoulders of my dinner jacket up over my neck, picked up a copy of the *Star* someone had left in a shop doorway and held it over my head, and traipsed off towards Rathbone Place. While I went I thought about the last time I'd gone catspawing for Haversham and what a —— disaster that had been. It had turned one by the time I got home—the place was as quiet as the grave and all the other lodgers had gone to bed—but there were a couple of letters on the mat that must have come by the evening post, so I pulled them open and chucked them on the bed.

The first one, which was addressed to me in my own handwriting, was from the *New Statesman* turning down a poem I'd sent them a month ago. Not looking at the poem, which fluttered out onto the floor on its single sheet of paper, along with a message in dainty italic printed on a funereal parchment slip which said, '*The editor regrets that he is unable to accept the proposed contribution*', I picked up the second letter and stared disbelievingly at it.

Dear James,

I am so sorry that I had a headache the other evening and could not accept your kind offer of a drink. It was very kind of you to be so understanding. I hope that we can see each other again soon.

Yours most truly,
Gladys Marlborough

Well what do you know? For a moment I forgot about the patter of heels behind me in Dean Street and the little chap with the slicked-back hair emerging out of the shadows of the pub door. I've had enough letters from women in my time to know when I'm being strung along, and on the face of it this didn't seem to be one of them. On the other hand, there was something going on here that I couldn't for the life of me fathom. For some reason I didn't feel like going to sleep after that, so I made myself a cup of tea and sat by the window watching the drunks weaving round the dustbins, and trying to write another poem that had come into my head the day before. That's the thing about being a writer, I find. You have to take your opportunities where you find them. The drawback, as I've invariably found, is that every so often other people's opportunities take you somewhere you had no intention of going.

6

JUST THE KIND OF MAN
WE NEED

Blackshirt boys wear whipcord trousers
Roll-up pullover tops
Wrinkle their noses at Jewish voices
Wanting time to stop.

James Ross, Soho Eclogues

'I really cannot apologize enough, Mr Ross, for what happened.'

'That's quite all right, Mrs Wisbeach.'

'And Mr Laal, of all people.'

'We all make mistakes.'

'I blame myself for not listening to Mr Warburton. He told me that he had been to a se— a gathering where Mr Laal had communicated with the spirit of the lady's deceased husband, and then when he went home afterwards he found that it was exactly what had been written about the deceased in *The Times*.'

'It must be a very difficult job.'

'And then poor Miss Marlborough. What must she have thought of us?'

'I expect she'll get over it.'

It was the day after the evening I'd ended up in West End Central, and I was sitting in Mrs Wisbeach's front room, teacup balanced on my lap, and a rock bun on the occasional table beside me. I'd come in search of the fifteen bob that was owing, but to Mrs Wisbeach it was clearly a heaven-sent opportunity to relieve her feelings about Mr Laal and the hank of butter muslin. Not that I was complaining, naturally. I'd got two cups of Pekoe Points inside me, and I was looking forward to a third.

'It was very good of you to invite Gladys—Miss Marlborough—to join us, Mrs Wisbeach,' I piped up. As I've said before, it's my experience that old ladies like deferential heartiness from us young fellows, and this one seemed to be lapping it up.

'Oh yes, Miss Marlborough.' Mrs Wisbeach looked a bit thoughtful. 'A delightful girl. Very modern, of course.'

'I suppose she is, rather.'

'And such a lot of callers coming to visit her. At such odd times of the day, too.'

'Is that right?' I wondered who the callers were and what they came calling about.

'But a delightful girl. Do you know, she has offered to look after Hercules one afternoon next week when I have to visit my sister-in-law in Reigate? I call that very neighbourly.'

I took a squint at Hercules, who was slobbering away at my trouser bottoms, and thought that Gladys was welcome to him. I hadn't seen her since I'd got the letter, but I was planning on going up there after I'd finished with Mrs Wisbeach.

'Now, you mustn't let me keep you, Mr Ross,' Mrs Wisbeach said. 'I'm sure you have a great many calls on your time.'

Well, that was true enough. It was ten past eleven, and so far I'd only done a couple of houses in Meard Street and one in Wardour. Officially I did two streets a day, working from nine to one and

86

dodging back to places where there'd been nobody in every half-hour or so in the hope of catching them. Still, I was getting the hang of this rent-collecting business. Essentially the requirements were just the same as selling vacuum cleaners or carpet lotion, or any of the other things I've done in my time: persistence, cheek and not minding if anyone cut up rough once in a while. Plus attending to any little foibles that the people you call on are itching to tell you about. Already that morning I'd inspected a model of the *Lusitania* that an old chap had made out of match-stalks and volunteered 'saucer' as the solution to 'Cup-bearer' (6) which was 17 across in that morning's *Daily Telegraph* crossword.

'Thank you for the tea, Mrs Wisbeach,' I said with maximal heartiness. 'Now, I wonder if I might trouble you for that thirteen shillings?'

'Well, if you're absolutely sure that you spoke to Mr Samuelson about that window frame?'

'I certainly have, Mrs Wisbeach. And he told me to tell you that he'd give it his urgent attention.'

It was more or less true.

'Then here you are, Mr Ross.'

I stowed the thirteen bob away in my trouser pocket, tore Mrs Wisbeach's receipt out of the book and handed it to her, gave Hercules a surreptitious prod up the backside with the toe of my boot and breezed out onto the landing. So far so good. Ten feet away there was radio music coming out from under the door of Mr Sibierski's flat, so I banged on the door a couple of times. There was nothing doing, though, so after I'd smoked a fag and wondered at the extraordinary amount of mouse droppings they had on the stairs I made my way up to the second-floor back.

Two minutes and half a dozen knocks later I was just telling myself that she wasn't there and starting to head off down the stairs when the door jerked open and she put her face out onto the landing. She was wearing the dressing gown again and a pair of harem slippers, and didn't look too pleased.

'Oh it's you,' she said, when she saw me. 'I thought you were the milkman. What do you want?'

'I was just passing,' I said, a bit lamely. A chap needs encouragement, you see, when he's parked on a girl's doorstep, and not just to be told that she thought he was the milkman. There was a nasty moment when I thought she was going to send me on my way, but then she gave a little twist of her head, pulled the door open a bit wider and said: 'You'd better come in.'

The flat was even dirtier than last time, I noticed. There were two or three gardenias wilting away in murky glasses of water, about a dozen copies of the *Sketch* strewn all over the sofa, and washing drying on a hanger. Plus someone had left a plate of sandwiches on the floor that had begun to curl up at the corners.

'I got your letter,' I said, as I sat down in one of the armchairs, next to a saucer on which lay, of all things, a stick of Brighton rock.

'What letter?'

'The one you sent me a couple of days ago. About being sorry you'd had a headache and couldn't go out after we'd been to Mrs Wisbeach's.'

'That old cow,' she said. 'Do you know, I said I'd look after her bloody dog next week when she's away visiting her sister-in-law?'

'She told me,' I said. 'She thinks you're a

88

delightful girl.' I didn't say anything about the callers.

'Christ,' she said. I didn't know whether she was still complaining about having to look after the dog or didn't like being called a delightful girl. 'Do you want a cup of tea?'

I had about a pint and a half of Mrs Wisbeach's best Pekoe Points inside me, but this was too good an offer to turn down. 'I'd like one very much.' There didn't seem any point in beating about the bush, so I said: 'Do you like the theatre?'

'It depends what's on.'

'West End plays?'

'I don't mind.'

I'd had keener responses in my time, but I pressed on. 'Only I've just been made dramatic critic of the *Crucible*.'

'Is that a magazine or something?'

'It comes out every month. Well, most months. You must have seen it in the shops. Anyway, I've got two tickets for *Silver Wedding* next Tuesday night.'

'What's that about?'

I tried to remember what Mortimer-Smith had said in his note. 'It's about this couple who've been married for twenty-five years. And then the husband goes off with the wife's best friend. Or hang on, the wife goes off with the husband's best friend.'

She was pouring water from the kettle into the teapot by now, with a look of absolute disdain on her face—the kind of look Boudicca might have given as she stepped down off her chariot onto a mound of corpses.

'All right. I'll come. When'll it be over?'

'Ten. Half past.'

'Only I've to be at work at the club by eleven.'

One thing I noticed that had changed since my last visit was that the bunch of dead roses had been cleared away.

'How's Dennis?' I asked.

'I don't know,' she said vaguely. 'I think he's gone away somewhere.' She didn't seem especially put out that I'd asked. 'Here's your tea.'

*   *   *

By the time I'd finished the tea and was back out in Meard Street it was nearly twelve. The wind had got up and there were herring-coloured clouds scudding westward instead of the pale sky that had been there an hour before. I wasn't due at the Toreador until the evening, so I figured I might as well head up the King's Road and see what was doing at the Black House. Whatever happened, I could at least tell Haversham I'd been spying out the land. Fact is, though, as the bus crawled down Regent Street I felt properly miserable in a way I hadn't done for ages. The odd thing was, I couldn't work out why. There I was, with money coming in for a change, dramatic critic of the *Crucible*, off to the Imperial on Tuesday night with the sulkiest blonde you ever saw in your life on my arm, and still there was something nagging at me that I couldn't put my finger on. Someone had left a paper on the seat next to mine with a story on the front page about a chap who'd married his third wife and had the first two turn up at the church to forbid the wedding, so I browsed through that for a bit and felt better, while the bus nosed on down Piccadilly and in the direction of Sloane Square. What with the lunch-hour coming on there were plenty of people about—blokes with expensive faces looking out from bowler hats as they marched off into Birdcage Walk, touts lounging outside the sentries' boxes at the palace gates, a file of kids from one of the smart prep schools going two by two down the road to Victoria—and I stared at them for a bit, thinking that it was funny how life turned out, and how most of the things you wanted to do weren't worth doing when you finally got round to them.

The Black House turned out to be at the far end of the King's Road, stuck between some shops and a pub that looked as if it had seen better days. I was all for heading into the pub, but then I remembered Haversham sitting at the desk in West End Central with his eyes swivelling in his head and reckoned I'd better not hang about. It was a big old barrack of a place that looked as if it had been some kind of institute, with a set of iron railings out the front, a sign that said BRITISH UNION OF FASCISTS—LONDON UNIT on the wall, and a couple of pasty-faced girls in black blouses and calf-length skirts swabbing away at the steps as if the Lord Mayor was due to inspect them ten minutes later. Nipping past them into the hall, where there were a couple of chairs, a portrait of the king and a picture of Mosley in fencing gear looking as if he'd just sat on a tack, I came across a bloke in a grey apron with a fag tucked behind his ear pushing a broom over the tiles.

'Help you, son?'

'I should like to join your organization,' I said.

Oddly, he looked a bit flummoxed by this. Perhaps you were supposed to apply in writing or turn up at one of the meetings you saw advertised

91

in the papers. One of the girls, who'd been sluicing the steps with a pail of water, sent me a haughty look and I said to myself: Wait till you see me in a pair of whipcord trousers and a black jumper.

'Want to join, eh?'

'That's right.'

'Best thing would be to see Mr Baxter. He's the man you want.'

'Where's he then?'

'Down that corridor. Up the stairs. Fourth door along. Unless he's gone out, that is.'

I set off along the corridor. There was no one about. At intervals there'd been posters stuck on the walls about preparing for action and the red menace and pictures of tweedy young chaps and their girls enjoying a hike in the country. As Haversham had said, it was all a bit like the Boy Scouts, only without the knots. The fourth door along the upstairs landing was half open, and a balding chap with horn-rimmed glasses and buck teeth was writing something at a desk.

'Are you Mr Baxter?'

'That's right. What can I do for you? If it's that cistern leaking again, then I'm afraid it's a matter for the porter.'

'I should like to join your organization . . . sir,' I added. This went down well, as I'd intended it to, and Baxter positively jumped to his feet. I thought he was going to shake my hand in his enthusiasm, but in the end he just hovered a couple of feet away darting me appreciative looks, a bit like a farmer eyeing up Buttercup Horniman the Third in his pen at the agricultural show. Here's another one who never got over having to say goodbye to the officers' mess in 1918, I thought—he was wearing a Toc H tie, too—and sure enough he bawled out: 'Name?'

'Ross, sir.' And for good measure I added, '40157G.' It wasn't my army number, but he was never going to know.

'Ah. Ex-serviceman, I see.'

I explained about the hut on the South Downs where I'd sat steaming open the mail with Corporal Hackett and mooning over the nurses who went by on errands to the village and he nodded his head.

'Just the kind of man we need. Occupation?'

Somehow I didn't think collecting rents for Sammy in Meard Street and standing in the vestibule of the Toreador saying, 'Evening, sir,' and 'Evening, madam,' would go down too well, so I threw back my shoulders and said: 'Journalist, sir.'

'Even better. We need all the propaganda merchants we can get. Anyone who could vouch for you? I'm afraid we've had one or two chaps trying to join us under false pretences.'

And I'm one of them, I thought. But then I had a perfectly brilliant idea. 'My uncle, sir. I believe he is the secretary of your Ramsgate branch.'

'Is he? Good show.' Baxter looked so delighted at this that I was worried he'd haul me straight off to Sir Oswald as an example of the kind of talent they were attracting these days, but after he'd written down Uncle George's address in a file he calmed down a bit and started prosing on about the weekly meetings and the fund-raising drive that the leader was so keen on.

'When should I report for duty, sir?'

'Eh? Well, let me see, there's a meeting for new members on Thursday. Perhaps you could come to that. I daresay a lot of it will be old hat to a chap like you, but some of the young fellows don't have the experience, if you catch my drift.'

'But is there anything I could do now, sir? It seems a pity to come all this way'—it was only a couple of miles, but I figured there was no harm in letting Baxter think I'd trekked in from Outer Mongolia—'and then go straight back home again.'

As I'd anticipated, this went down like a dozen oysters. A candidate for the novitiate genuflecting in the Mother Superior's sitting room couldn't have made a better impression.

'Not much to do at the moment, I take it?' Baxter said.

'Precious little work to be got, sir,' I said, and then added for good measure, 'what with all these foreigners coming and taking the bread out of our mouths. If there's a job for me to do here, then I'd like to get started.'

'Good show,' Baxter said. 'Well, I think the best thing would be for you to come down to the drill square and meet a few of your fellow volunteers.'

And so we breezed off, him leading the way, me deferentially following, down through the bowels of the building to a largish room in the basement about the size of a village hall. On the way we passed two or three blokes bustling about inscrutably on errands who, when they saw us, threw absolutely slavish looks and bawled out, 'Good morning Mr Baxter!' as if he was the Chief of the Imperial General Staff on his way through the Cabinet Office door. In the drill hall there were a couple of trestle tables, an upright piano pushed into a corner, and a tea urn beside which eight or nine chaps in overalls and tennis shoes stood hopefully loitering. Baxter stopped to eye them up, and it was exactly like my old PT master, Mr

Ackroyd, coming across a couple of sixth-formers he suspected of smoking cigar ends in the lavatory block.

'Now, what are you fellows doing?'

There was an uncomfortable collective stir, like troubled dreamers coming temporarily awake, and a little man in horn-rimmed spectacles who couldn't have been more than five foot tall said: 'We're waiting for Mr Abercrombie's unarmed combat lesson, sir.'

'Unarmed combat, eh?' Baxter said, with a look so appreciative that he might have been sniffing a soup tureen. 'Ah, this must be Mr Abercrombie coming now. Well, carry on.'

While he stopped to have a word with Mr Abercrombie about the fire buckets, I took a look at the band of noble companions I'd fetched up with. The average age, I reckoned, would have been about forty, and there were a couple of older chaps who looked as if they'd been lining the streets at the Golden Jubilee. All the same, there were a couple of likely lads with lantern jaws and big bruisers' faces lounging near the tea urn for whom you suspected any lessons in unarmed combat would be pretty much superfluous.

'All right you men, fall in,' Mr Abercrombie bawled out, once the business of the fire bucket had been conclusively settled. He was a foxy-looking character in a tracksuit who clearly came from somewhere like Macclesfield and had pretty obviously ruptured himself at some point in his career. 'No, not like that!' We'd instantly assembled in a line that stretched the width of the hall. 'Double rows.'

So we shifted around a bit as directed, with the

little man with the horn-rimmed specs and one or two others at the front and the two likely lads and myself at the back.

'Now then,' Mr Abercrombie said. I looked at his feet, expecting to see gym shoes, but for some reason he was wearing an enormous pair of hobnailed golfing brogues. 'The first thing I'm going to teach you is how to fall correctly.' At close quarters his accent sounded more Macclesfield than ever. 'Now, if I asked you'—he indicated the little man in the spectacles—'to fall on the point of your shoulder, you'd break your collarbone. What would you do?'

'Break my collarbone, Mr Abercrombie,' the little chap meekly replied.

'So you would,' Abercrombie said. 'No doubt about it. Six weeks with your arm in a sling and no good to man or beast. Now, the trick with falling is to cushion yourself as you go down. Doesn't matter how hard the surface is, just lean into yourself as you go and you'll be A1. Just watch me.'

He went down dramatically on the point of one shoulder. You could have heard the bone crack outside in the King's Road.

While they were carting Abercrombie off into another room, and someone had gone to telephone for a doctor, I got talking to the little man in the horn-rims, whose name was Blennerhassett.

'You're not in your uniform then?'

'Oh we don't wear them on informal occasions,' Blennerhassett said. He was a nice, friendly chap. 'How unfortunate that Mr Abercrombie should injure himself.'

'Yes, wasn't it?'

'Only he'd promised to show us how to

96

immobilize your assailant by using pressure points.'

'I'm sorry to have missed it,' I said.

Privately I was wondering if this mightn't be a good time to plead a pressing engagement elsewhere and skedaddle. But no, barely five minutes after Abercrombie had been dragged off, a big burly chap arrived in the hall who was clearly intending to carry on where he'd left off.

'My name's Hardcastle,' he said. 'What's happened here?'

If Abercrombie could just about have passed for a gent, then Hardcastle had pretty clearly spent most of his professional life on the parade ground at Catterick.

'He had an accident, sir, and had to go off to the doctor,' Blennerhassett explained.

'Did he now? Well, how far did you get with him?'

'We'd just got to the point where you fall down and break your collarbone,' I said.

The likely lads grinned at this, but Hardcastle seemed not to notice. Anyway, for the next half-hour he had us jumping about pretending to kick each other in the shins and tumbling over whenever anyone jammed on our insteps. What I couldn't help noticing was the varying degrees of enthusiasm on offer: Blennerhassett and the two older chaps fairly flailed away, as if they were entered for an all-in wrestling championship at the Queen Elizabeth Hall the very next week, while the likely lads frankly slacked. With the memory of Mr Abercrombie's fate to guide me, I spent most of the time retying my shoelaces and dodging swings from Blennerhassett that wouldn't have inconvenienced a five-year-old. All this time, and for Haversham's benefit as much as my own, I was trying to work out what I thought about the Black House and the atmosphere that prevailed in it. From one point of view, of course, it was merely hilarious, with Blennerhassett and his pals marching around as if they were a grown-up version of the Boys' Brigade. But I had a feeling that the likely lads at the back didn't just see themselves as overgrown Boy Scouts. No, they were looking for trouble, and no mistake.

By the time we'd finished I was in a proper lather, and grateful for the cups of tea that were handed out. While we were drinking them, I got talking to Blennerhassett.

'What line of work are you in?'

'Chartered accountant with Cooper Brothers in Gutter Lane,' he said. 'Know the firm? I've been with them twenty years.'

'Won't they be missing you?' I asked.

'It's my annual leave,' Blennerhassett said seriously. 'I thought I ought to do something useful with it this year, instead of us going to Great Yarmouth with my wife's mother. Though between you and me, I'd be better off looking at the ledgers than practising unarmed combat.'

'Less talking in the ranks there,' Hardcastle said, not quite humorously. 'I've orders to take you gentlemen off to the post room.'

It sounded harmless enough to me, but the likely lads let out no end of a moan—they clearly wanted to be off down the East End to hit Jews on the head—but Blennerhassett explained that 'post-room duties' meant sorting out leaflets and, if you were unlucky, having to deliver them as well, or at any rate hand them out to passers-by in the King's

Road.

'Sound move,' I said, thinking that I ought to be showing a bit of enthusiasm. 'The more propaganda we send out, the better we ought to do. How else are we going to shake the country up, I should like to know?'

Blennerhassett looked a bit doleful and said, yes, I was bang right, propaganda was the only way to do it these days, but although he'd do his best, he really didn't think he was cut out for trips along Whitechapel High Street with a pile of leaflets about the Red Menace stuffed in his knapsack. And it struck me that Blennerhassett was much more of a danger than the meaty boys of the second row. It's the people who feel they have to do their duty that you have to watch in affairs like this, you see. Likely lads just want to hit people and go home, but to the Blennerhassetts of this world it's a moral crusade. And that's where the trouble starts.

As I might have predicted, that's where the trouble started here. By the time we'd sorted the leaflets out—it was the usual stuff about international financial conspiracies and conniving Jewry—the clock was ticking on to one and there was a general movement in favour of knocking off for lunch. The likely lads, in particular—their names, I discovered, were Caraway and Stevens— were all for disappearing to a pub in World's End. But Blennerhassett said that we ought to go straight out into the King's Road and distribute them. Baxter, who appeared in the room on his way out somewhere—probably lunching with the Home Secretary to judge by the goofy look on his face—agreed with him, and the upshot was that Blennerhassett, yours truly and the two older chaps ended up on the steps of the Black House with a box of leaflets in each hand and instructions not to come back until they'd all been disposed of. If it had been left to me, I'd have chucked the boxes down the nearest grating and skedaddled, but Blennerhassett had one of those intent, serious looks on his face that reminded me of the Inversnecky magistrate when the town drunk is hauled up in front of him each Monday morning.

'The best thing to do, I think, is to divide into pairs,' he proposed. 'Graves and Osborne, perhaps you wouldn't mind doing the far end, and Ross and I will see how we get on here.'

Have you ever stood on a street corner handing out leaflets to the passing throng? As a matter of fact I'd done this before, back in the old days on the South Coast, with Mrs Bence-Jones waiting for me in the Europa Tea Rooms, but it had always been vacuum cleaners or cut-price groceries, not the international financial conspiracy and the Jew bankers. Plus it had started to rain again, and the water was already dripping down the back of my neck. To make matters worse, there's a look that comes into the eyes of people you hand out leaflets to, one that says, *I may be down on my luck, chum, but nowhere so down as you*. We'd been given some advice by Baxter on what to do if anyone started asking questions, but as you might imagine this was worse than useless. I hadn't been on the job more than five minutes before a heavy-set woman who looked as if she ought to have been coaching lacrosse in a girls' school seized a leaflet, stared at it as if it were a pornographic tract, and demanded: 'Are you some sort of political canvasser?'

'We represent the British Union of Fascists,

madam.'

'Is that Sir Oswald Mosley?'

'The very same, madam.'

'He should never have left off being a Unionist, if you want my opinion.'

'I'm very interested to hear it, madam.'

I glanced over my shoulder, to where Blennerhassett was having a terrific argument with an off-duty bus conductor—he still had his badge on his lapel—about the League of Nations. There were one or two tough-looking chaps hanging about in the vicinity of the bus conductor, and I was just wondering whether a stroll down to the other end of the street to see how Graves and Osborne were getting on mightn't be a sound scheme, when the bus conductor picked up half a dozen of the leaflets Blennerhassett was holding, chucked them on the pavement and started stamping on them. 'There!' he said. 'That's what I think of your Sir Oswald f——g Mosley.' Blennerhassett had started to say something in return—I think it began 'Well, really . . .'—when all of a sudden a car came sharking up out of nowhere and out jumped three heavies in full Blackshirt gear—roll-neck pullovers, corduroy breeches, the lot. There was a flash of silver as one of them swung his fist—knuckleduster, I thought—and the bus conductor went staggering away across the pavement. The toughs melted away, and the chap who'd swung the fist stood with a foot on the car's fender while the ever-dutiful Blennerhassett bent down to retrieve the trampled leaflets.

'Thanks very much,' I said to the knuckleduster merchant.

'Pleasure,' he said. 'Often get a rough crowd in the King's Road.'

101

And that, I thought, as he stood there flashing his teeth, was the third time I'd seen him. The other two times had been chucking the brick through the window of the Toreador and leaning out of the shadows in Shaftesbury Avenue to beckon Gladys into the pub.

7

MATINÉE PERFORMANCE

Say hello to Dot and Elspeth
Nod to the chap with the cauliflower ear
Cut down Frith Street into Old Compton
Here in the autumn of the year.

James Ross, Soho Eclogues

I was sitting in the Café Polska with a cup of coffee
growing cold at my elbow, watching the tarts go up
and down Berwick Street. On the hoarding beyond
the far pavement they'd put up one of those metal-
plate Guinness ads, but the rain had got into it
and the toucan had almost rusted away. The queer
thing about watching the tarts prowl up and down
Berwick Street, I'd decided, was that it took you
ages to work out who was on the game and who
wasn't. You'd watch a girl with one of those sullen,
come-hither expressions slink out of a tobacconist's
shop and stare hopefully into the distance, only for
a fresh-faced fellow who was clearly her cousin or
her young man to step up and claim her. I once saw
a woman who looked as if five minutes earlier she'd
been doing the fan dance before a riotous audience
at the Folies Bergère be enthusiastically greeted by
a clergyman in a soft hat and an Old Marlburian
tie. On the other hand, perhaps she really was a
tart. You can never tell, you know, and the crossest
I ever saw Mrs Bence-Jones was the time when a
chap came up to her on Bognor seafront, bold as

brass, and asked if she was looking for business.

Although you couldn't tell a tart straight off, you could always tell the men who were after them in twenty seconds flat. They all had the same kind of look—sort of desperate and furtive at the same time—and their intentions were so obvious they might just as well have had calling cards woven into their hat brims. I was watching one of them now: a little, rat-faced character with an attaché case under one arm, who looked like a Methodist preacher up from Swansea, off to do a little whoring on the QT instead of attending convocation at the Wesleyan Hall. He'd started off staring into the shop windows. Then he'd settled on sentry duty next to one of the market stalls. A girl in an olive mac and heels tripped by—it wasn't raining but the sky was a dull grey colour—and he made a little feint in her direction, got the brush-off and drifted away in the direction of a lamp post where a Soho regular called Spring-heel Jack, who had one leg shorter than the other but kept it up with a sort of iron spike, was talking to the cats' meat man. Finally a motherly looking woman, who I'd have taken for a publican's wife out shopping, came and detached him from the crowd in exactly the same way that a collie cuts a sheep out of the flock and they went off companionably together towards Oxford Street. It was all very odd.

There were two reasons for me sitting in the Café Polska, by the way, with a cup of coffee going cold at my elbow and the butts of half a dozen Park Drive clogging up the ashtray. One was that I'd arranged to meet Haversham here to give him an update, only he was twenty minutes late. The other—connected to the first in a way—was that

104

I badly wanted some time to sit and think about Gladys. I knew I was dead gone on her by this time, you see—it was that sulky look she had when she stared at you—but at the same time I knew hardly anything about her, and the things I did know didn't inspire too much confidence, as my form master used to say when he came to write my end-of-term report. The pretending to have a headache and then being seen sprinting up the street five minutes later to meet a chap in a pub I could cope with—most women do that if you give them half a chance—but what about if the man of her choice spends his time lobbing half-bricks through nightclub windows and sails into punch-ups in the King's Road waving a knuckleduster?

As I was pondering the implications of all this there was a terrible, ground-down sigh about a foot away from my head—the kind of sigh Richard III probably gave at Bosworth when he realized the nearest horse was three fields away—and I looked up to find Haversham a couple of feet from my shoulder. He looked even madder than ever, which is to say that the skin near the top of his head was reddish-coloured and abraded and his eyes looked like a couple of black stones at the bottom of a goldfish bowl. He sat down heavily in the chair next to mine and had Jan, the old waiter, fetch him a cup of tea.

'Business not too good?'

'B——y bad, I'd call it,' Haversham said. He tried to light a cigarette with a match from a box of Swan Vestas, but the head of the match broke off and burnt him on the cheek.

'What's the matter?' I asked.

'That b——g prince again,' Haversham said.

105

He'd got the fag going by now. The tea came and he stared at it.

'What's the prince gone and done?' Most of the time when you read about the Prince of Wales in the newspapers it was about him falling off horses and breaking his arm. What he'd done to annoy Haversham I couldn't imagine.

'He's putting us in a deuced awkward position, that's what he's doing,' Haversham said mournfully. 'You'd think the heir to the throne'd have more consideration for the police force.'

'How's he putting you in an awkward position then?'

'Turning up at nightclubs we're supposed to be closing down,' Haversham said. 'Take last Tuesday night. Word comes through we're to do a raid on the Pandora in Frith Street. Every by-law in the book been broke, apparently. Licence not been renewed. Serving drinks after eleven to them as hasn't ordered food. Commissioner jumping up and down to see justice done. We got there at eleven-thirty. Tip-top do it was and all. The Hon. Mrs Pelly doing the Sir Roger de Coverley with Lord Mountfichet. And would you believe it, 'is Royal Highness had left half an hour since! What about it if we'd gone in there at ten, eh? It don't bear thinking about.' He took a long swig out of his cup and grimaced. 'This tea's p——, too,' he said. 'I dunno when I've tasted worse. Now, what have you got to tell me?'

So I explained about the morning at the Black House, the unarmed combat lessons and Gladys's boyfriend, who'd been so free and easy with the silverware, while Haversham smoked another cigarette and arranged a dozen sugar lumps in the

106

shape of a Maltese cross.

'That's good work, that is,' he said once I'd finished. 'A1. But what we need's a name, see? You'll have to go back and make enquiries. Find out who he is.'

'How am I supposed to do that?'

'That's your lookout,' Haversham said. He had this horrible way of patting you on the head and then virtually telling you to start from scratch again. 'But it's good work, I grant you. Wonder if he's the chap who bust up old Slattery's place in Wardour the other week.'

'What was all that about?'

'Oh, two blokes smashed up one of those shops as sell smut and French letters under the counter. Broke the till open, too, by all accounts and then took off towards Oxford Street. Half a dozen people saw them do it, but not a witness statement worth writing down.'

There was something nagging at me while he was saying this, and when he stopped and had another draw at his fag I remembered what it was: the trail of asphalt footprints leading up from Wardour Street and off into Rathbone Place and the entrance hall to my digs. How about if the two things were connected? After all, people don't go sprinting through asphalt unless they've got a very good reason, do they? For a moment I wondered about letting Haversham in on this, but then I decided that I'd keep mum, on the excellent grounds that the less hold he had over me the better.

'Anyway,' Haversham said—he looked horribly depressed, like a chap I'd once seen a picture of in the *News of the World* who'd got eight score draws

107

on a Saturday night, marched into work to tell the boss what he thought of him and then gone home to find that his wife had forgotten to send in the coupon—'you go and have another look-see in the King's Road. Soon as I've got a name and address we can say goodbye and no questions asked.'

Until the next time that is, I thought to myself—we'd had another conversation like this a couple of years back. 'Right you are,' I said brightly, but thinking that if there was one thing I'd like to get shot of it was Haversham's ugly mug and his black-olive eyes. I watched him move off down Berwick Street, thinking that whatever difficulty anyone might have in telling a tart from a respectable girl, no one would take more than five seconds to work out that Haversham was a plain-clothes policeman.

It was about half eleven by now, and by rights I should have been in Bateman Street with Sammy's receipt book under my arm seeing if Mrs Bolsover, who'd turned off the radio and declined to answer the door last time I'd called, could be taken unawares. But there was something else I wanted to think about, and this was the logistics of the next ten hours. It was the day I was supposed to be taking Gladys to the theatre to see *Silver Wedding*, but just the other night I'd had a note telling me it was the day she'd volunteered to look after Hercules while Mrs Wisbeach was off seeing her sister-in-law, and couldn't we go and see a matinée instead? I couldn't see any problem about this, although it would mean an afternoon off the collecting. On the other hand, I reckoned I could redeem myself by working a shift at the Toreador between nine and midnight. It'd be an exhausting day, but fortitude is what we Rosses are all about.

I was still thinking that it might be a good idea to go and see if I could winkle a few bob out of Mrs Bolsover when another thought occurred to me, and instead of heading south from the Café Polska I nipped off into Wardour Street. There was no trouble finding Mr Slattery's shop, which had one of its windows boarded up. In addition, there was a patch of newly tarmacked pavement close by with three or four bootmarks trodden into the surface. The shop looked such a dreary, flyblown kind of place that you wondered why anyone would want to bust it up, but I noticed that the books on the shelf next to the door were definitely on the warmish side, so you never know. Personally, I always find books with titles like *High Jinks in a Parisian Convent* a terrible let-down, but then I'm such a trusting sort of a chap. Anyway, the distance between the top end of Wardour Street, across Oxford Street and then into Rathbone wasn't more than a hundred yards. Whoever'd turned over Mr Slattery's shop could easily have legged it there in under a minute.

By this time I was standing in the entrance hall to my digs staring at the door where the trail of asphalt had come to a halt. Even now—you could tell how often the place got swept—there was a pebble or two rolling across the floor. Now, the kind of person who has digs in Rathbone Place keeps themselves to themselves, you understand, and I'd been there six weeks without exchanging so much as a word with any of the other tenants, except a chap on the third floor who I'd lent the end of a tin of boot polish to when he wanted to smarten himself up for a waiter's job he was going for. Some people had their names scrawled on a

109

piece of paper above the door handle, but this was stone blank. There was a pile of uncollected post on the sill just inside the main door, so I picked it up and started leafing through it, but you could tell that it had all been lying there for months or had simply been delivered to the wrong address, and somehow I didn't reckon that the chap who'd smashed up Slattery's shop was likely to be the Honourable Algernon Partington-Bruce, whoever he was. Anyhow, I hung about for ten minutes or so, but there was nothing doing, and in the end, having assured myself that this particular vantage point would repay further study, wandered off to Lew Levy's for a cup of chicory essence and a bacon sandwich. I might have had a pay rise, you see, but precious little of it had come in yet. Besides, I was taking Gladys to the theatre, and I figured I'd need the thirty bob I had in my pocket in case of emergencies.

Anyway, 2.30 saw me marching along Drury Lane as per our arrangement, and there she was, bang on time, waiting on the theatre steps. This seemed so extraordinary, in the light of our previous dealings—my previous dealings with practically any woman, if it came to that—that I suppose I must have looked a bit startled, because the first thing she said after we'd nodded at each other was: 'Aren't you pleased to see me?'

'Of course I am. Why shouldn't I be?'

'You look a bit odd.'

'Do I? I can't imagine why.'

She, by the way, was looking a million dollars, with a red beret on top of one of those ultra-fashionable raincoats you see the mannequins wearing in the Bond Street windows. Even better,

I got the feeling that she was there because she wanted to be, which was no end of a confidence-booster. Anyhow, we simply sailed up the steps past the commissionaire, who was so impressed by the 'You be d——d' glance I threw him that he practically abased himself on the spot, sped across the quarter-acre of red carpeting and presented our passes to the chap at the gate. And that's where the trouble started.

'What's these then?' he demanded, once he'd turned them over in his hands and squinted at them like a bank-teller with a couple of forged tenners.

'I was given to understand,' I remarked, a touch on the haughty side, 'that they're complimentary tickets to this afternoon's performance.'

'Well they're not,' said the flunkey. There was a bit of queue already building up behind us. 'They're tickets for tonight. Look. Eight o'clock it says, not three.'

'I don't you think you quite understand,' I said. Gladys, I saw, had stopped taking any notice of us and was staring at the ceiling. 'I'm the dramatic critic of the *Crucible*. I'm supposed to be reviewing this production.'

'No can do, chum. You and the lady'll have to come back tonight. That's about the long and short of it.'

I decided it was time to wheel up the big guns, so I put on my toniest accent and said: 'Look here, my man, I think the best thing would be if I spoke to the manager.'

'It's the manager's afternoon off.' There were a dozen people behind us now, all taking a keen interest in the proceedings.

'Isn't there anyone else I can see?'

'You can see Mr Maclintock if you like. He's the manager's assistant.'

Mr Maclintock sat in a little cubbyhole next to the ice-cream stall. I left Gladys kicking her heels in the foyer and looking none too pleased.

'What can I do for you, sir?'

'There seems to be a problem with these tickets.'

He whipped them out of my hand. 'No problem that I can see, sir. They're for tonight's performance. Not this afternoon's.'

'Look,' I said. 'I'm reviewing this production for the *Crucible*. This is the only time I could get here.'

'No press seats on a matinée day, sir. They used to come in straight from the pub, fall asleep and start snoring. These days we let the Chelsea pensioners in instead.'

By this time, I reckoned, Gladys would probably have given it up as a bad job.

'Look,' I said again. 'We're men of the world. I've a particular reason for wanting to see this afternoon's show. Promised my young lady. You let us in and I'll make it worth your while.'

'A quid.'

'Fifteen bob's all I can afford.'

'Right you are,' he said.

'What about the Chelsea pensioners?' I asked.

'They don't always come,' he said. 'In you go.'

By the grace of God, Gladys hadn't stormed off in a huff, though she looked what my Aunt Marigold would have called a trifle discomposed. Mr Maclintock called the flunkey back and had us taken upstairs to a pair of seats in the balcony. There were even a couple of programmes thrown in free, and with the five bob change from the quid I nipped out and bought a box of Caley's chocolates from one of the usherettes. The theatre was still filling up, and we sat there for a while watching the crowd file in—they were mostly oldish women in fur coats with even older men to steer them into their seats and apologize to the people they'd bumped into on the way. I was just thinking that things were improving no end—Gladys had actually consented to eat a couple of the chocolates and ask whether the portrait on the wall behind us was of Sir Henry Irving—when, lo and behold, the woman sitting next to us went chalk white, clutched her midriff and started bringing up her lunch over the seat in front.

This went on for what seemed like hours, with usherettes offering assistance and the woman (who I suspected of being half-cut) protesting that, no, she was fine and then doubling up over the seat again, until finally they hauled her away, leaving one hell of a mess and an indescribable stink. Fortunately there were two more empty seats down at the end of the row, and after a great deal of pushing and treading on people's toes we managed to dive into them just as the house lights went down and the curtain started to rise. While all this was going on I took several looks at Gladys and discovered that she was one of those girls—I'd come across them before—who at moments of crisis simply switch off and let the person they're with deal with it. No doubt about it, if the old girl had attacked us with a machete instead of parting company with a dozen oysters Gladys would just have stared bleakly over the rail at the people in the stalls until someone arrived to clean up.

Anyhow, the play started soon after that, which reminded me that I was there in a professional

113

capacity and couldn't just sink back in exhaustion and stare at Gladys through the murk. As it turned out, I'd forgotten my notebook, but the programme had a blank page at the back, so I made do with that. In fact, it was quite a decent play, all about this chap who'd been married a quarter of a century to a woman who looked as if she wouldn't say boo to a goose, wondering whether the grass wouldn't be greener on the other side, talking it over with his best friend, only to have the best friend die unexpectedly, after which they turn up a letter in his effects declaring how ashamed he is for having betrayed the chap by . . . Well, you can guess the rest. Anyway, the great thing was that Gladys seemed to like it too. At any rate, when the moment came when they opened the letter—it was all very dramatic, with the chap's old mother going off in a dead faint—she gave a little shriek and clapped her hands together, just as she'd done when the planchette went into action. All the chocolates had gone by now, so I reckoned that, what with the studious look I'd put on while scribbling notes on the programmes (dead highbrow notes they were, too, things like 'situations unresolved' and 'essential plasticity'), I hadn't made too bad an impression.

When we came out into Drury Lane it was near enough five, halfway to dusk and the rain was coming on again.

'What shall we do now?' I asked. There was at least another three hours until I had to put in an appearance at the Toreador.

'I've got to go back and see to Hercules.'

'When's Mrs Wisbeach coming home?'

'I don't know. Later on, I expect. But I said I'd give the wretched thing its supper.'

'Shall I come with you?'

'I don't see why not.'

No doubt about it, things were looking up, as the moment she said this a taxi lurched into view, and by leaping off the kerb and cutting out another chap who'd clearly had his heart set on it I had the two of us installed in the back seat before you could say 'Clarence Atry'. It would mean breaking into the solitary quid I now had in my trouser pocket, but I wasn't complaining. In my experience if there's one thing women like it's having a chap summon taxis on their behalf. Netta had always been at her most gracious in taxi queues. The other thing is that if you take a girl home in a taxi, it increases your chances of being asked inside.

I'd been worried that Hercules would have taken advantage of her absence by chewing up the sitting-room carpet or relieving himself on the sofa cushions, but no, all he'd done was distribute various bits of that morning's *News Chronicle* around the hallway. When he saw us he started up the most tremendous racket, but clearly he hadn't reckoned with Gladys, who opened up a kind of broom cupboard to the side of the kitchen and simply bundled him inside.

'If we're going to have a cup of tea,' she said, 'it won't be with that b——y thing in the room.'

'What about his supper?'

'I don't know. I'll get it in a bit.' I couldn't tell if she'd gone off into a sulk or was just normally exasperated by Hercules.

'Did you like the play?' I asked.

She thought about this. 'I didn't not like it.'

I was itching to ask her about the chap who'd been waiting for her outside the pub in Shaftesbury

Avenue, but something told me this wasn't the right time. We hadn't yet turned the electric light on and the flat had this odd, aquarium-like quality, so that it wouldn't have seemed wonderful if a shoal of fish had suddenly swum up out of the kitchen and started nosing around in between our feet. In the broom cupboard Hercules was making odd yodelling noises and whinnies of disquiet.

'I'll get some tea,' Gladys said. 'Why don't you put the fire on?'

So I lit the gas, which gave a kind of exhausted pop and promptly went out, and put a bob in the meter to get it working again, while Gladys knocked the tea things about in a way that suggested serious bad temper but which, I'd now assured myself, was simply the way she was. It had been exactly the same that morning I knocked on the door and she thought I was the milkman—not rudeness, but a kind of fundamental fury about everything. I've known several girls like that and it's a question not so much of self-absorption but what a French poet I once knew called 'the poetics of life'. Fact is, I could see Gladys's point entirely. Girls like her are made to have cups of tea brought to them, not to have to make it themselves, and if they were living a thousand years ago they'd have had the head cut off the person who brought it into the bargain.

When she came back with the tea tray she said, as if it had only just occurred to her: 'I thought you were a pansy.'

'Why was that?' I'd had worse insults.

'I don't know. You talk horribly posh sometimes.'

'It's my public school education,' I said.

'Pansies always go on about their public school educations.'

116

'None of the ones I knew ever did.'

'If you went to a public school, why've you a job as a rent collector?'

It was a good question, which had been asked quite a few times before. I decided to say what I usually said. 'Writers need to see a bit of life.'

In my experience when a girl tells you she used to think you were a pansy it means not only that she's changed her mind but that she'd like convincing proof she was right. Anyway, I went across and put a hand on her arm, got a furious green-eyed stare in return, which in nine cases out of ten would have seen me out on the landing a minute later, but for some reason ended up with the two of us on Mrs Wisbeach's sofa while Hercules—conscious that something was going on from which he was purposely excluded—howled like a banshee.

'A pansy wouldn't do this,' I said.

'No, he wouldn't.'

'Nor this, either.'

'I suppose not . . . here.'

Quite how long this went on, and what might have been the upshot of it, I couldn't begin to tell you, but all of a sudden—just as I'd begun to think that of all the girls I'd ended up on sofas with this had been the fastest worker—there was a noise of footsteps on the landing and the sound of a key turning in the lock.

'Christ!' Gladys said.

'What is it?'

'It's Mrs Wisbeach. Quick . . . give me those.'

If I'd had any sense I'd have tried to brazen it out, said that Miss Marlborough had just asked me to mend a fuse or something, but for some reason I lost my head completely, jumped to my feet, looked for a refuge, couldn't find one, and then, finally, just as Gladys went haring off to the vestibule to welcome home Mrs Wisbeach, threw open the door of the broom cupboard and squeezed myself inside.

You'd have expected Hercules, who I nearly fell over as I tugged the door shut, to go bananas, but curiously enough he just dropped his head and started sniffing at my ankles. I was so grateful for this that it barely crossed my mind that the first thing Mrs Wisbeach would wonder was where he was. Meanwhile, I was looking to Gladys to make a fine old and potentially exit-concealing fuss of her as she came into the flat.

'Did you have a nice time at your sister-in-law's, Mrs Wisbeach?'

'I must say, Evangeline is getting very *odd* these days. Having her dining room painted that queer colour. What Francis would have said had he lived I can't imagine . . . But, my dear, wherever are your shoes?'

'Oh, aren't I wearing them?' Gladys said, a bit too artfully for my liking. 'I suppose I must have felt more comfortable with them off.'

'And has Hercules been a good doggie? Where is he?'

'I think he's a bit tired, Mrs Wisbeach. Last time I looked he was having a sleep in the corner of your bedroom.'

'In the *bedroom*? How very odd.'

The voices were moving out of range, which was my cue to get out of the flat sharpish. Luckily Mrs Wisbeach's bedroom was off the corridor two doors down. If I didn't make a row I could be out of there in ten seconds. As to what Gladys was going to say about Hercules being locked up in the broom

118

cupboard, well, that was her lookout. I nudged the door open a crack just to make sure my ears hadn't deceived me, but the only thing in view was Mrs Wisbeach's handbag, which she'd plonked down on the table. Here goes then, I thought, pushing open the door, at which Hercules raised his nose off the floor, gave a howl fit to wake the dead and took a chunk out of the lower part of my calf. Naturally it hurt like hell, and for two pins I'd have given him a boot in the ribs. On the other hand I didn't want Mrs Wisbeach's charge sheet to grow any longer, so I lowered my head, sprinted over the carpet to the front door, which happily had been left on the latch, and hurled myself out onto the landing, where I sat down in a heap clutching at my leg and listening to the fusillade of barking coming from inside. If anybody wanted to come out and see what I was doing there, well they were welcome to.

After a bit, when I'd inspected the damage—not as bad as it looked, I reckoned—and limped off down the stairs into Meard Street, I started to see the funny side of it. After all, if anyone had any explaining to do it was Gladys, whom Mrs Wisbeach would automatically assume had been up to some funny business. Mind you, old ladies will believe practically anything, in my experience, if you put it to them respectfully enough. What would she say? That Hercules had started foaming at the mouth and she'd had to lock him in there for her own safety? That he'd gone after a rat? If I knew Gladys, it'd be something pretty plausible. Fact is, though, all this reminded me just how little I knew about her, and in particular her dealings with the King's Road hooligan, and by the time I'd wandered off into Dean Street I was properly sobered up. It was only about six—far too early for work—and what with the excitements of the past half-hour my nerves were in one hell of a state. Isn't there a poet who talks about the throb and hum of a mind well taxed? Well, that was how I felt as I trudged back to my digs, so much so that I practically got run over by an electric brougham that some damn fool was urging along Oxford Street and had to be rescued by an old chap with a row of medals on his chest who was playing the harmonium for coppers under a street lamp.

Back at Rathbone Place the hall was empty, and I reckoned a really smart operator would have knocked on the door of the ground-floor room and seen who answered. But I wasn't feeling a particularly smart operator just then, so I mooched on up the stairs, boiled some hot water in a kettle, poured it into a tooth mug with some liniment out of a tube that happened to be lying around, and then swabbed away at my leg with a handkerchief. Curiously enough, the first thing I set eyes on while I was doing this was that letter Netta had sent me, lying half-hidden under a pile old *New Statesman*s, and it's a mark of the state I was in, I suppose, that I pulled it out and started reading it. What would Netta've made of Gladys? I wondered. One was a vicar's daughter from Frinton who worked as a commercial artist, and the other was a sulky blonde from a nightclub, but I reckoned they'd find things in common. You'll think it odd, perhaps, but one of my regular dreams involved all the women I'd ever known sitting round a tea table comparing notes.

My leg had stopped hurting so much by now, though it still looked badly swollen, and what I

120

really wanted was a square meal and a stiff whiskey, but there was no food in the place, bar the half of a loaf of bread which looked suspiciously as if a mouse had been at it, and no drink save a bottle of light ale that had gone flat, so I had to make do with a cup of tea. The really odd thing, though, was that there was a line or two of a poem knocking around in my head, and by the time I'd finished the tea the thing was near as dammit done. It wasn't half bad, either, all about the rain falling over the street lamps on an autumn night, and this chap who's torn between two girls, neither of whom likes him very much anyway, and a line about someone holding bitter-lust pressed flowers to their heart.

There was still an hour until I had to be at the Toreador, so I looked out the gold-nibbed pen I used to write with and some of the Basildon Bond paper Netta had given me—there was only a sheet or two of it left—and copied it out, wrote 'TO NETTA' on the top in outsize capitals, stuck it in an envelope and went out to post it in the box on the corner of Oxford Street. By rights, I suppose, I should have waited until morning to see how it looked. But then I've always been an impulsive sort of chap, and there are times when you have to go where the spirit leads you. What Netta would say when she saw it, though, I couldn't begin to think. Then I thought about all the other poems that pen had written and all the people they'd been addressed to—Mrs Bence-Jones back in Hove, and Ethel, and Susie, who'd given me the runaround that time I was selling the carpet-cleaning lotion, and Richenda who was CP and thought that poetry was a decadent art form—while the light grew blacker in Rathbone Place and the noise of the buses tearing down Oxford Street sounded like tumbrels in my ears.

Part Two

8

TIME OUT OF MIND

Tea and two slices cost fourpence
A kipper on toast is a shilling
And afterwards step down to Greek Street
To see if the ladies are willing.

James Ross, Soho Eclogues

Naturally, when I woke up the next morning—a bit on the late side—I was in the most tremendous stew. And as if the memory of the previous night wasn't enough to be going on with, I discovered that the top of my calf where Hercules had sunk his teeth into it had turned a purplish colour. Worse, the *London Mercury* had sent back a poem which I'd reckoned would knock anything T. S. Eliot had ever written into a cocked hat. On the plus side there was a letter from Tommy Kilmarnock asking me to come round and see him soon as convenient, and this cheered me up no end, as Tommy was a tip-top divorce lawyer with a list of West End clients as long as your laundry bill and the jobs he put my way usually paid cash in advance.

It was nearly twelve by the time I got round to his chambers, which were in one of those flyblown squares between the Strand and the river, and his clerk said he was out seeing a client but he'd left instructions to ask: would I mind waiting? Well, I hung about in his office for a bit, read the line of invitations on his mantelpiece, which were mostly to parties in Belgrave Square, browsed through one or two of the juicier cases in the *Law Gazette*—it's surprising what those society women will say about the husbands they're getting shot of—and at about half past he breezed through the door wearing a twenty-guinea suit and smoking an outsize cigar that practically needed a tripod to rest on.

'How's business?' I asked as he plonked his things on the table, told the clerk to fetch two stiff whiskies and looked at a telegram that had just come in from the Duchess of Westmorland.

'Not so bad. Terribly immoral lot these days, you know, the upper classes.'

I nodded at the line of invitation cards. 'Will you be going to the Countess of Kinnoul's *thé dansant* next Friday week?'

'Bessie Kinnoul? No, I've chucked. Lavinia Sutherland's asked me to one of her beanos at Claridge's.'

As you can see, Tommy had come a long way since he was junior clerk to Messrs Sheldrake & Finkelstein in the Hackney Road. There were some papers on his desk which he'd pulled out of a file marked 'AA', and when he'd looked at them for a while and told me about various mutual acquaintances, none of whom were exactly distinguishing themselves in the world, he said: 'Doing anything this evening?'

I explained about the front-of-house engagement at the Toreador, but Tommy shook his head. 'That's OK,' he said. 'I'll fix it with Sammy. He owes me a favour. Now, how would you like a little trip to the seaside?'

'Where to exactly?'

'Ramsgate. Down in Kent.'

126

He had both hands splayed out over the front of his waistcoat and the Old Carthusian tie, which I had a pretty good idea he wasn't entitled to, and looked a bit like Mr Toad practising his victory speech.

'What do I have to do? It's not one of those fake co-respondent's jobs is it?' I'd been this way before, down in Brighton with an actress called Constantia Fenwick, and got into no end of trouble.

Tommy gave a little twitch of exasperation. 'Nothing a man of your capacities can't cope with. Just obtaining the evidence is what we need. You ever hear of a character called Arthur Aitchison?'

Actually I *had* heard of Arthur Aitchison. He was a northern comedian who'd been on the halls for the best part of a decade, and he had a song that went: 'I started courting a smashing fan-dancer/To marry her, that was my plan/Now it's all off with the smashing fan-dancer/She fell down and damaged her . . .'—well, you can guess the rest.

'The Skelmersdale Chappie? The Mad-hatter with the Patter?'

'That's the one, I think.' You could tell Tommy never went out much in the evenings. 'Well, his wife's divorcing him.'

'Why's that then?'

'Search me. *Cherchez la femme*, I suppose. We've got it down as "wantonly unreasonable behaviour liable to undermine the plaintiff's mental stability". Anyway, he's agreed to do the decent thing, so someone's got to go down to Ramsgate and collect the evidence.'

It was the usual put-up co-respondent's job, you see. Tommy would have hired some hot tomato to occupy the bedroom next to his in the hotel,

127

Arthur'd saunter along there at six o'clock in the morning, and the chambermaid'd find them both there when she brought in the breakfast an hour or so later.

'Why Ramsgate?' I asked.

'He's on at the Palace Theatre there.' Tommy looked at the notes on his desk. 'With Annette and Durno, Olly Aston and his Empire Melody Masters and Six Yuk Ching's Chinese Wonders. Anyway, there's ten quid in it, and I said I'd get someone down there tonight.'

'What about the girl?'

Tommy hoicked another piece of paper out of the inner pocket of his suit jacket and stared at it. 'She's called Florence Risborough. Get down to Charing Cross by four and she'll be waiting by the flower stall.'

Well, ten quid was ten quid, even with all the other backsheesh that had come my way just lately. Plus, there's a side of me that always likes staying in swanky hotels. It's what us Rosses were born to, you see.

'Where'll I be staying?' I asked.

'The Grand. Down by the seafront. I'll wire and reserve you a room.'

'What's the dinner allowance?'

'Christ!' Tommy said. 'You can have pheasant in oyster sauce for all I care, with *marrons glacés* to follow. Just bring me a receipt.' I was hoping he'd stand me lunch, but Tommy was an inhospitable beggar sometimes, and in response to my hopefully enquiring look he simply cut the top off another cigar and said he'd got work to do, so I sauntered back into the square, where the rain had started coming down again, and wondered what to do with myself. It was only a quarter to one, and I didn't have to be at Charing Cross until four, so I figured that before I collected my stuff I'd call in on Mortimer-Smith at the *Crucible* office. Curiously, now I'd got the next twenty-four hours sorted out, with the prospect of ten quid at the end of it, I'd practically forgotten about Gladys and the BUF and my dates with Haversham. Not that I didn't have a shrewd suspicion that the cupboard I'd stowed them away in wouldn't spring open the moment I got back.

Anyway, I went and ate a cheese roll in a Lyons on the corner of Fleet Street and Chancery Lane, took a bus up to the top end of the Tottenham Court Road and then headed west down Warren Street looking in the windows of the used car places as I went. Now I came to think of it, what with the job from Tommy and the *Crucible* and the extra from Sammy, I reckoned I might be able to afford a little bus myself in a month or two's time. I had a vision of driving Gladys down to Maidenhead for dinner at the Berengaria or maybe further along the river for tea at Skindles, which I'd always been told was about the classiest place on earth for a chap to take his girl.

By the time I got to Fitzroy Square it was about a quarter to two. Mortimer-Smith was leaning back in his chair with one foot on the desk in exactly the same way as I'd left him last time. There were review copies all over the floor and the second of the room's chairs was covered in proof sheets.

'Everything OK?'

'Could be better.'

'Mona's parents been kicking up again?'

'Between you and me, I don't think I'll have any

more trouble in that quarter,' Mortimer-Smith said. 'She showed them the tickets I'd got to the Chelsea Arts Ball the other day and they didn't bat an eye. It just shows what you can do when you try. No, it's Chalkie.'

'What's he been doing?'

'Sticking his oar in,' Mortimer-Smith said. He ran a hand through his thinning grey-brown hair, which had been cut *en brosse* and, together with his moustache, made him look as if he ought to be running an *estaminet* on the Left Bank.

'But all proprietors do that, don't they? Even Jimmy used to complain that the chap who owned the *Blue Bugloss* was always trying to get his wife's nature poems into the verse supplements.'

'Nature poetry I could put up with,' Mortimer-Smith said. 'In fact, it's an underrated genre. I've always thought we could learn a lot from Whitman. But have a look at this.' And he shoved a wad of manuscript over the desk at me. It was called *The Theosophist's Challenge: A Symbiosis*, and might have been thirty pages long.

'It's not short, is it?'

'No, it's not short.'

'Who's Professor Battycharya?'

'B——d if I know. But if Chalkie thinks I'm going to start putting in stuff about Madame Blavatsky he can take a hike. That kind of thing is out of date.'

'Could you just tell him it's too long for the mag?'

'Chalkie says he's prepared to pay the extra printing costs.'

'Tell him you had an expert read it and Professor Battycharya's talking through his hat.'

'It's worth a try, I suppose,' Mortimer-Smith said, not sounding specially convinced. 'How was *Silver Wedding*?'

'Seen better.'

'Perhaps you'll have better luck with that Communist thing in the Whitechapel Road where they try and hang the tallyman from the lamp post. At any rate, it'll make a nice change from the theosophist's challenge.'

It had just gone two by now, and I doubted whether Mortimer-Smith would have wanted a drink even if I'd been prepared to stand him one, so I wandered back to Rathbone Place, looked out some clothes and then sat there reading a copy of *Cage Birds* that had somehow made its way into the room, where they were still going on about whether you ought to feed rapeseed to bullfinches. A bit after that I set off for Charing Cross, where the rain had cleared but it was still deuced cold, with little shafts of wind blowing off the tarmac and scraping your face like sandpaper.

Curiously enough, hanging about waiting for someone you don't know at a railway station never ranks at all high on my list of cushy numbers. Come four o'clock I was parked by the flower stall, as per Tommy's instructions, but there was no one about and after a bit I reckoned that Miss Risborough must have made a mistake and gone off to stand somewhere else. There was a blonde piece powdering her nose under the clock who looked every inch a co-respondent's honeypot, but she turned out to be waiting for her brother, and a dark-haired girl I'd blithely accosted next to the W. H. Smith threatened to have me in charge. Finally, when I'd trekked back to the flower stall—it was gone ten past by now—I noticed a suety-looking number in a cloche hat with a suitcase in one hand shoot me a sardonic glance.

'Are you Miss Risborough? I'm Mr Ross.'

'I've been waiting here ten minutes,' Miss Risborough said. She clearly had trouble with her aitches. 'B——g train goes at twenty past.'

You'd have thought that the girls they got to do co-respondents' jobs would all come from the same shop, so to speak, but no, they were always different. Some of them looked as if they'd just strolled out of Lady Colefax's drawing room, and some of them looked as if their last paid engagement had been selling matches in Seven Dials. There'd been one who'd been educated at Cheltenham Ladies College and in toting her bag off the rack had asked me if I'd mind helping with her reticule. Anyway, this one was definitely from the Seven Dials end of the market. There were several holes in her stockings and her make-up looked as if it had been laid on with a paintbrush.

'I've got the tickets,' I told her. 'D'you want a porter for that case?'

'Not when I've got you to carry it, thanks.'

There was a queue at the ticket office, and by the time I got back she was sitting on her suitcase eating a pork pie out of a paper wrapper.

'It's seventeen past,' she said.

'You'd better get off your —— then' I said. Usually I treated girls with a gentlemanly courtesy, but I'd already decided this one was the limit. There was something else nagging me, which was a suspicion—faint but insistent—that I'd seen her before somewhere. The Toreador? But she didn't look like the kind of girl Sammy would have given

132

legroom to. One of the cafés I hung about in? That didn't seem likely either. So where was it? In the end, what with the bother of shifting her suitcase and tearing through the gate just as the porter tried to tug it shut, I put it at the back of my mind and concentrated on making it to the train on time, which we did with half a minute to spare, chucking our bags onto the rack and ourselves into the seats with such groans of exhaustion that the old girl on the far side of the compartment—a grey-haired character who looked as though she taught Classics in a girls' school—sat up as if a swarm of bees had suddenly poured out of the ventilation shaft.

'Christ!' Miss Risborough said. 'I've had just about enough of this game.'

The queer thing was that after this she perked up no end, accepted the offer of a cigarette and made herself comfortable, and within ten minutes of the train setting off she was talking nineteen to the dozen. All to do with status, if you ask me, and wanting to impress your personality on the inferior party in the transaction. When I wasn't listening to her complaining about her bunions, which were playing her up no end, or the landlord of her digs, who was in the habit of giving her a 'funny look', I stared out of the window where the twilight was sinking in and the London suburbs rushed by in the gloom. England's hell in autumn. The lights go on earlier and earlier, the fog seeps into the field-bottoms and the horizon in the early morning looks like a fish's underside. Have you ever looked at a London crowd in November? The men are all worrying about whether they'll get sacked before Christmas, and the women are all wondering if that half-pound of scrag end will make a stew on

133

its own or'd be better used to eke out last night's shepherd's pie. And the bald heads and the fat, dropsical legs! Never mind the little wisps of smoke from hundreds of individual fags—all of us have our private storm cloud hanging over our head, and it won't be gone until spring marches round again, and sometimes not even then.

Anyway, some of this must have communicated itself to Miss Risborough, because just as we were rolling through Penge or one of those dreary north Kent suburbs she stopped talking about her feet and said: 'You're a gloomy one, aren't you?'

'No I'm not. I'm just introspective.' It's what I usually said, and sometimes people believed it.

There was a sharp whiff of grease as she tore another pork pie out of its wrapper. 'Isn't it Arthur Aitchison we're going to meet?'

'That's the one.' I was still trying to work out where I'd seen her before, and not getting anywhere.

'I saw him the other month at the Holborn Empire.'

'Any good?'

'I don't like those northern chaps. Can't understand what they say.'

'So who do you like then?'

'I like Harry Tate when he does "Peacehaven". But really I like chaps that sing.'

I bet you do, I thought. But she was a friendly sort. Peckish, too. By my reckoning, between Charing Cross and Ramsgate she put away another two pork pies, a Scotch egg, a packet of potato chips and a paper bag full of boiled sweets. The old girl opposite wasn't even pretending to read her copy of Alec Waugh's *Hot Countries*, and simply

134

stared at her, eyes agog.

By the time we got to Ramsgate, the dusk was crawling up out of the fields, there was rain belting in against the carriage windows and you could see the distant white shapes of gulls whirling in the blue-back sky. It was about half past five, but the station was halfway to empty; the first batch of City workers wouldn't be in for another hour.

'Do you do this job a lot?' I asked.

'Now and again. That's if the money's all right. How much are you getting?'

'Six,' I lied.

'Six? That's a pound less than me. You ought to look out for yourself, you ought. Never let yourself be taken for granted, that's what I always say.'

'I'm sure you're right,' I said. 'Know where the Grand is?'

'It's about half a mile away. Top end of the front. I came here once with my young man.'

'Here's your taxi then.'

'Ent you coming with me?'

'No offence,' I said. 'Wouldn't look right if we turned up at the same time. Besides, I've got to find Aitchison. Now, you enjoy yourself.'

'Oh, I will,' she said. By this time I was positive I'd seen her before. 'I always do. A nice piece of fish, if there is any. Not to mention a good night's sleep with no man's b——y great feet pushing you about.'

She really was from the Seven Dials end of the market and no mistake. There was another taxi waiting at the rank with an old boy behind the wheel who looked as if he'd probably driven Lot home from Gomorrah, but in the end, and despite the rain, which was coming down in streams, I decided to walk. There's nothing like spying out the land, you see, when you're fetched up in a strange place. As it turned out, Ramsgate was a frost— nothing but pebble-dash villas and chaps in carpet slippers coming out with umbrellas over their heads to buy the racing finals. After a bit I popped into a tobacconist's shop and bought a copy of the local paper, which was full of the most yawn-inducing stuff about cat burglars and how much they'd raised at the Conservative whist drive, and consulted the by no means very extensive 'The week's events in Ramsgate' column. It turned out that the Palace only ran to a single house midweek, so I reckoned Aitchison would be back at the Grand sometime after eight. That left a couple of hours to kill, so I mooched along the front for a while—it was all shut up now, and the fastening on the gate of the funfair clanked in the wind—had a quick one at a pub called the Bosun's Delight, which suggested that the Ramsgate bosuns were pretty easy to please, got into conversation with a chap I met who reckoned that most of Shakespeare's plays had been written by Ben Jonson, and then strolled up to the Grand just as the town hall clock struck eight.

Do you know those out-of-season provincial hotels, I wonder? This one looked more dead than alive, which was to say that half the selections on the dinner menu had been crossed out and the girl at reception had her knitting out on the desk. Still, they seemed pleased to see me and, after I'd signed the book, I sauntered along to the bar. I'd only just settled myself at one of the corner tables when a little chap in a violently checked suit with thinning hair and a face that looked like a plate of scarlet porridge came barrelling into the room.

'Are you Mr Aitchison?'

He gave me the kind of look that the vermin man at the Toreador used to give before he went down to the cellar. 'Happen I am.'

'My name's Ross. I was supposed to meet you here.'

'You from the press?'

'No, I'm from the solicitor's office.'

'And what about Dolores or whatever her name is? Is she here too?'

'I think she's up on the third floor.'

'Well, she'll get to see me before too long I daresay.' It occurred to me that he'd already had a fair amount to drink. 'I've done this before, you see.'

'What? Got divorced?'

'That's right. Up in Blackpool one summer season. The tart we were paying to do the honours never turned up, so I had to make do with the chambermaid.'

The curious thing, I noticed, was his accent, which had started off in broad Lancashire but now seemed more like cockney.

'No offence,' I said, 'but you don't sound like Arthur Aitchison.'

'I can see you're a bright lad,' he said. 'All that Lancashire stuff is a try-on. Audience likes it, you see. Thinks it's 'omely.'

'So you're not the Skelmersdale Chappie?'

'I went there once,' Aitchison said. His face had lost the bantering look it'd had when I introduced myself and gone intent and serious. 'Awful place. All ruddy Catholics to a man, women wearing shawls, kids with no backsides to their trousers. D'you know, they drink tea out of bowls? You never

137

saw anything like it. Here,' he said—he obviously saw me as a kindred spirit—'you eaten yet?'

'No.'

'Well, come and have supper. It'll be a nice change from the Israelite who owns the Palace telling me the takings are down and why don't I go on third after the Chinese plate-spinner.'

Pretty soon we were sitting in the restaurant with a bottle of Chablis open on the table between us and the waiters hanging over our shoulders as if we were a couple of crowned heads down on a sightseeing trip. He'd have been about fifty, I suppose, and it didn't take more than five minutes of his conversation, which was mostly about women, to see why the first and second Mrs Aitchison had wanted to get shot of him.

'You're a young chap,' he said, out of nowhere. 'I expect you've seen a bit of the world. Now what do women want?'

Actually it was a question I'd often pondered. The ones I'd known had wanted all sorts of things, ranging from refurbished fishermen's cottages in Winchelsea to a Drage's three-piece and a leather cover for the *Radio Times*, to 'respect', whatever that was, and a whole heap of minor courtesies that went under the general heading of 'treating a lady in the manner to which she is accustomed'. What they hadn't seemed to want was yours truly, but that wasn't something I could decently tell Aitchison.

'It's a very interesting question.'

'You're telling me.' As well as the wine, he had a double whisky that he'd brought from the bar and every minute or so his hand would curl round it as if he half expected someone to take it away. 'Now, take my Eunice.' (He pronounced it

*Oo*nice.) 'What does she want? If I take her out to a restaurant she'll tell me she'd sooner eat at home. If we stay at home, then she'll say she wants to go out somewhere. If it's a nice 'ot day she'll say she's dying for a lick of wind, and then when the first of September comes round she'll start moping over the summer that's gorn. So what does she want? Blowed if I know.'

'You been married long?' I asked. Some of the chaps who worked for Tommy reckoned they got bored by the clients' habit of always talking about themselves. Myself, I couldn't get enough of it.

'Ten years. Of course, it was her idea.'

'Was it?'

'That's right. I was on the northern circuit for Moss Empires, and she used to follow me. I'd be on at Leeds, Manchester, Rochdale, Salford, anywhere north of the Trent, and she'd be there sitting in the second row.'

A waiter came over and hovered respectfully. Aitchison picked up one of the dinner menus that we'd been idly looking at.

'You got any lobster?'

The waiter looked a bit cautious. 'I believe there is lobster, sir.'

'Well, bring us a couple then . . . And some potatoes.'

'Potatoes, sir?'

'That's right. Lots of potatoes.' The waiter nipped off sharpish. I can't say I blamed him. Aitchison looked around the table, a bit wildly, as if he wondered where he was. Then he said: 'Where was I?'

'You were telling me about your wife before you were married. About how she used to come and see you on the northern circuit.'

'That's right. So I was. Even then, though, I couldn't understand what she wanted. Do you know, not long after we got married—a Sunday morning, it was, just after breakfast—she turned round to me and said: "I don't like you being on the halls. It's common, that's what it is. Why can't you be an auctioneer?"'

Uncle George had worked for an auctioneer once in the Midlands. It was one of the many things that the Old Lady had against him.

'It's not a bad trade,' I said.

'Well, it's a curious thing, because if you'd have asked me thirty years ago "What do you want to do?" I'd have said: a chap as stands up at a lectern with a gavel in his hand knocking stuff down to the highest bidder.'

By this time the lobsters had arrived. There were little hammers to get the meat out of the claws with. Aitchison picked one up and swung it at his plate as if he were trying to demolish a wall. There was a kind of cracking noise and a couple of ounces of melted butter sprayed out all over his shirt-front.

'B——r!' Aitchison said. He didn't seem too put out. I took a squint round the room at the dozen or so diners who were regarding us with unfeigned horror. They included a couple of old ladies with grey sausage curls in black evening dresses and a fat chap who looked like a bookie treating a woman who clearly wasn't his wife to veal escalopes.

'Never got the hang of this,' Aitchison said affably—he'd clearly taken a shine to me, but then people do sometimes. 'Anyway, thing is I've been through this half a dozen times before.'

This seemed a bit excessive, even for

140

showbusiness. 'What? You mean you've been divorced six times?'

'No fear! I mean, Eunice keeps on instituting proceedings and then changing her mind. I always go along with it. I don't know why. Perhaps it gives her life a bit of excitement. You'd be surprised how late she leaves it, too. Why, one time I was sitting in the lawyer's office with my pen out waiting to sign the form and she rushed in and says, "Arthur, don't do it or I won't be answerable."'

'What did she mean by that?'

'B——d if I know. She's a very emotional woman, you know. There was one time when this pal of hers was staying that she thought was giving me the eye, and she chucked a suitcase full of her clothes out of the window.'

I looked down at his plate. Somehow, without my even noticing, he'd got through most of the lobster and a stack of potatoes they'd brought him in a kind of porcelain bucket. The potato dish caught his eye and he said: 'Funny sort of thing to serve potatoes in, don't you reckon? Looks more like a chamber pot . . . Christ!'

The two old girls in evening dresses had given up any pretence of eating their cutlets and were just staring at him.

'What's the matter?'

'What did I tell you?' he said. 'It's her.'

There was a big, brassy-looking woman of about forty, with black hair done up in elaborately marcelled waves, standing in the doorway with her eye moving round the room as if she were auditioning for a part in *Cannibal Queen*. There's a girl you wouldn't cross in a hurry, I thought to myself. Sure enough, as soon as she saw the two of

141

us she heaved over like a battleship cruising into port. The chap who looked like a bookie blinked at her as she sailed past.

'Who's this then?'

As Aitchison looked as if he'd been struck dumb I said: 'My name's Ross.'

'What's he doing here?'

You could practically see the cogs whirring round in Aitchison's skull as he sized her up. 'Now look here, Eunice,' he said, a bit wearily, 'don't take on. He's from the solicitor's.'

'Oh Arthur,' Eunice said. 'Gorn and left me and never so much as a wave.'

'I think you'd better excuse me,' I said, starting to get up from my chair. They both ignored me.

'Now don't take on,' Aitchison said again. 'It was your idea in the first place.'

'Only because I was driven to it.'

'Who's driving you anywhere, I'd like to know?'

I looked round when I got the door, and you could see that here was another case that wouldn't be getting anywhere near the divorce courts. It was about nine o'clock now, and what with the excitement and the half-bottle of wine I'd put away, I reckoned I needed a breather, so I nipped out through the front entrance of the hotel and went and smoked a fag in a kind of shrubbery. In the distance I could hear the waves crashing down onto the beach: the wind was getting up. Turning cold as well. Back at the Marquis of Granby they'd be ordering up whisky and gingers and Mortimer-Smith would be telling everybody about Mona and what a grand girl she was. Mrs Wisbeach would be laying out the Tarot cards, most likely, while at the Toreador they'd be serving supper to the

142

early guests and wondering if 'Mr Gossip' from the *Sketch* was going to show. Meanwhile, here I was sixty miles away, freezing my —— off in the Kentish darkness and wondering how I could best pick up the fragments of the evening. The first thing I reckoned I ought to do was to see exactly what state Mr and Mrs Aitchison were in, so as soon as I'd finished the fag and smoked another one for luck I went back into the dining room, but the table we'd been parked at was empty and the waiter was clearing away the plates. He seemed a friendly sort, so I said: 'Gone for good?'

'Looks like it.'

'Say anything?'

'Asked for a bottle of champagne to be sent up to their room.'

'Nice work if you can get it.'

'Not my type.'

'Cigarette?'

'You're a toff,' he said, palming the fag and tucking it behind his ear in a single, continuous movement that made me think of the clerks in the accountancy firm at Hove when they reckoned the boss's eye was on them. The fat chap who looked like a bookie and his ladyfriend were piling into bread-and-butter pudding now as if they hadn't had a square meal in weeks. Seeing that Mr and Mrs A. were clearly embarked on a second—or maybe even a seventh—honeymoon, the next thing I figured I ought to do was to let Florence know that all bets were off, so a moment or two later I took the lift up to the third floor and knocked on the door. There was no reply, which in normal circumstances would have put me in no end of a tizz, but when I thought about it I couldn't have cared less. If Florence wanted to go gallivanting around Ramsgate in the pitch-dark then that was her lookout.

Meanwhile there was another little scheme in my head that had nothing to do with her, or the Aitchisons or even Tommy Kilmarnock, and I reckoned the morning would be a jolly good time to put it into practice. So I went off to my room, had room service bring me a double brandy—there's no reason to stint yourself on these occasions, you know—looked at a book that someone had left under the bed called *Hard-hearted Hannah* and then browsed through the Gideon's Bible I found in the bedside table until I came to the bit at the start of Ecclesiastes about the preacher saying vanity of vanities, all is vanity, and what profit hath a man of all his labour which he taketh under the sun, and one generation passing away but another coming and the earth abiding for ever, which was certainly true in my line of work when you stopped to think about it. Then I fell asleep and had a terrifying dream about Haversham frog-marching me through the state rooms at Buckingham Palace and telling me to look under the chamber pots in case anyone had hidden anything in them, while Gladys and Lord Beaverbrook set up a card table and started playing snap for fivers and the Old Lady sat on the sideboard and told Uncle George that his great-great-grandfather had been a cousin of the Earl of Midlothian and what did he think of that? It must have been the lobster.

9

RAMSGATE SANDS

The scent of dried roses
And powdered noses
Fox furs from Eli & Moses
Back-stage at the Embassy Club

James Ross, Soho Eclogues

I'd set the alarm for a quarter to six. When it went off the room was still black as pitch and the wind was blowing up a storm beyond the window, and I had one of those queer moments of disorientation when you don't know who you are, where you've fetched up or how you've got there. After a bit, though, I perked up and went and drew the curtains and looked out onto the beach, where the waves were coming in like nobody's business, had a wash and brush-up and then skipped off along the corridor to Florence's room. There was a light burning under the door, and after I'd knocked and been told to come in I found her sitting up in bed in one of those off-the-shoulder nightdresses the movie actresses used to wear until they brought in the Hays Code.

'You're not supposed to be here for another hour,' she said. 'Let Mr Aitchison and me get comfortable first.'

'He's not coming,' I said.

'Got cold feet, has he? I've had that happen a few times.'

'It's more complicated than that.'

It took a minute or two to explain the events of the previous evening. The wind blew against the window frames in a series of little thuds. The window had been left open a crack and the cold air rushing in made the electric light bob up and down. When I'd finished she said: 'All right if I order breakfast?'

'Be my guest.'

'Why don't you stay and have it with me? Never did like having breakfast on my own.'

Now, I know a come-on when I see one. It was like Millicent Carbury and the photo album all over again.

'No thanks,' I said, reaching for the door handle. There was something else worrying me, over and above the fact that a suety girl who was no better than she should be was making eyes at me over the bedcovers in a hotel in Ramsgate while we were supposed to be in the middle of a job: I'd finally worked out where I'd seen her before. There was no doubt about it. She was the girl that Gladys had come walking up Berwick Street with and then said goodbye to outside the Café Polska.

*   *   *

It was about six thirty now and there was grey light spilling across the corridors of the Grand—ghastly grey light that seemed to have a queer, secondhand quality, as if all the good stuff had been used up and what we were getting was the dregs from the bottom of the barrel. It was far too early yet for the scheme I'd cooked up the previous night, so I sat in my room for a bit, drinking glasses of water to try to shift the headache I'd acquired from last night's carouse with Mr A., and thinking about Gladys and what she was doing hanging about with a girl like Florence. I'm a fastidious chap, you see, and I've still got old-fashioned notions about girls. I'm not saying they should all be a week out of the convent, you understand, but there is such a thing as maidenly modesty.

Then, when the clock had ticked round to 7.15 and there were footsteps sounding on the stairs, while a few old blokes in overcoats emerged onto the beach to walk their dogs, I trekked down to reception, routed out a surly-looking clerk who'd clearly been making merry the night before at the Dog and Partridge and settled the bill, asked for Florence's—she'd had a tremendous time ordering up bottles of soda water—and paid that as well from the money Tommy had given me. I then went into the dining room and ate a kipper while a man at the table next to me confided to his friend—a stiff-looking chap who could have been the local vicar—that he thought he'd caught the clap and what ought he to do about it?

My scheme was to look up Uncle George: not because I particularly wanted to spend half an hour listening to him prose on, but because I reckoned it might be a chance to pick up some information on the cheap. After all, Uncle George was, or had claimed to be, secretary of the local branch of the BUF. And while I didn't imagine this meant there'd be letters from Sir Oswald arriving by every post, still there might be a hint or two as to what was going on at the Black House. At any rate I was sure Haversham would be mightily impressed by my initiative.

It was about 8.15 when I left the hotel—still early—with sad-looking chaps in bowler hats on their way to the station, boys on bikes delivering newspapers and packs of schoolgirls in fawn-coloured mackintoshes hanging around on street corners. In the end, after I'd read a copy of that morning's *Mirror*, which some early-bird had left sticking out of a waste-paper bin, and had a cup of coffee in a café that looked as if it hadn't seen a fresh coat of paint since Waterloo, and where three monstrous old women sat swapping scandal about someone called Mrs Mort, I fetched up on the beach.

The wind had dropped a shade now and the dog-walkers had mostly gone home, so I smoked a fag and brooded a bit about Netta, and why things hadn't worked out between us, and Gladys, and whether they ever would with her. I could still see the look on Gladys's face when we'd heard the sound of the key turning in the lock, and I couldn't decide whether it was relief or disappointment or one of those odd combinations—I'd seen them before—where a girl doesn't know what she wants but takes whatever turns up. Anyhow, come ten it had started to rain again so I picked up the suitcase, which I'd been sitting on while I thought about Netta and Gladys, and skulked off into the centre of town to look for Uncle George.

Uncle George had always given out that he lived in one of the posher bits of Ramsgate, but curiously enough there was no sign of Beesley Street—I'd had the address off the Old Lady, years ago—in any of the rows of genteel villas, all done up in pebble-dash and with names like 'Mon Repos' and 'Sailor's Retreat', that were set back from the sea. In the end, after I'd asked a butcher's boy who'd come cycling past with a mound of bloody packages on the tray in front of him, I tracked it down to a part of the town near a tanning factory. Number sixteen turned out to be stuck between a tobacconist's shop and a ladies' knitwear emporium, and from the look of it seemed to have been practically squashed in half. There was a sign on the door that said NO HAWKERS and a terrific smell of old cooking fat. Anyhow, where Uncle George wanted to live was his own affair, I reckoned, and what could be wrong with a dutiful nephew coming to visit his old uncle? So as soon as I'd put out the fag I was smoking I banged on the door like a bailiff on bonus money.

It took nearly a minute for Uncle George to open the door. He was wearing an old waistcoat over a crumpled shirt and hadn't bothered to put on a tie. Or shaved, either, by the look of him. He was carrying a half-empty milk bottle in one hand, and when he saw me he gave a little start, so that the bottle almost ended up on the doorstep.

'What are you doing here?' he asked, sounding none too pleased.

'I just happened to be in Ramsgate, Uncle George,' I said. 'On business,' I added, just to show I wasn't the kind of chap who raced down to the Kent coast in October on a whim. 'And I thought I'd look you up.'

'You'd better come in,' he said, again not sounding as if he liked the idea above half.

As I'd suspected, the front door led directly into the sitting room—the Old Lady would have died of shame if she'd known about it. Behind the half-open kitchen door washing hung up to dry over the oven. Trying to work out what the various contending smells were, I reckoned they were cat, camphor and, funnily enough, Parma Violets. Curiously, once he'd closed the door Uncle George seemed to cheer up a bit. There were a couple of chairs in the corner of the room, both of them covered with newspapers, and he pushed one over for me to sit on.

'What kind of business?' he asked.

'Legal things,' I said, which was more or less accurate, and then before he could enquire any further: 'Where's Elsie?'

None of us in the family had ever so much as set eyes on Elsie in all the years Uncle George had been married to her.

Again, Uncle George looked horribly ill at ease, as if asking a man where his wife was when you called round to see him was about the worst insult you could offer.

'She's gone out,' he said at last.

'Oh yes?'

'Shopping,' Uncle George said vaguely, still not looking at all happy. Meanwhile, I was casting my eye surreptitiously around the room, knowing that the Old Lady would want full details when I next wrote home. The astonishing thing was how much clutter Uncle George had packed into it. There was a kind of ziggurat of books over by the far wall, including Field Marshall Buller's memoirs in three volumes. At least one of the house's occupants, too, was tremendously keen on Staffordshire china, as there were half a dozen statuettes of Polly Peachum and the like dotted around the place. But none of this offset my original impression, which was of something not much above the level of a junk shop.

'Nice little place you've got here,' I said.

'I keep telling Elsie we ought to get a bigger house,' Uncle George said, a bit defensively. 'But she always says, no, she likes it here. Handy, too.' Something else seemed to occur to him, and he said, a bit fiercely: 'And then as soon as anyone knows you've got a big house they come round and start taking advantage. Keep yourself to yourself is what I always say.'

'And how's the BUF?'

I'd clearly said the right thing at last, as Uncle George positively bridled. 'Ah,' he said, 'we're working wonders. Seventy-three people we had at a meeting at the golf club the other day. There's talk of sending a contingent to Olympia before Christmas. Captain Annesley-Jones says he's never seen anything like it.'

For a moment I thought I'd tell him about my adventures in the King's Road, but then I reckoned it might be better to wait until Mr Baxter made his enquiries. After all, the way I'd planned it I wasn't going to be in the BUF for more than a month. Less if I could manage it.

'Not working at the moment?' I asked, which was a nasty dig to throw at a chap you've found answering his front door at ten o'clock in the morning, but I'd had some stick from Uncle George over the years and I couldn't resist it.

'Trade's a bit slack,' Uncle George said. I couldn't remember if he was still selling advertising space on the local paper or peddling insurance, and he didn't elaborate. 'Hang on,' he said—a bit friendlier now he'd got used to me being in his front room, where no other member of the family had ever penetrated before, 'I'll make you a cup of tea, shall I?'

151

'That'd be nice,' I said. And give me the chance to look at the pile of letters on the sideboard, I thought to myself.

As I'd expected, Uncle George took ages to make the tea. Even better, he shut the kitchen door while he was doing it, which meant that I had a free run of the sideboard. There was the most tremendous pile of junk. Some of the letters were nearly two years old, but the recent stuff was all at the far end. From it I learned that Uncle George's overdraft at the bank stood at £11 3s. 4d., that Elsie was spending a small fortune at a draper's shop called Whitgift & Pickering, who'd sent their bill in three times now, and that somebody was in urgent negotiation to buy a patented truss from a firm of surgical appliance manufacturers in Eastbourne.

I was about to give up in disgust when a thick, cyclostyled wad of paper lying under a handbag caught my eye. Sure enough, it was called *A Call to Arms*, had a picture on the front of some exceptionally weedy-looking Blackshirts hauling the Union Jack up a flagpole and, as far as I could make out, offered an enticing budget of news to cadet branches down in the provinces. The Westminster and Belgravia branch, I learned, had been smiting the Bolshevik menace by raising £7 10s. at a whist drive and the lady members had enjoyed a fascinating tour of Kew Gardens. Naturally, all this tickled me no end.

Just underneath it, though, next to a picture of an outsize valkyrie called the Honourable Miss Armistead-Trench receiving her attendance prize was a sub-head that ran 'Despatch Box', topped by the news that *Members and Subscribers will be interested to know that Operation Clean-Up has begun in the Soho district, with particular reference to Wardour Street, Brewer Street and Dean Street. Further information will become available when the project, which is of a very exciting nature, gathers pace over the coming months.'* I'd just read it for the third time when a mighty clatter from the kitchen and a kind of tearing noise as the door fell open advertised the fact that Uncle George had finished the tea and was bringing it in.

Uncle George always said that he liked a sergeant-major's brew, and this would have killed a platoon of them stone dead. It was near enough orange in colour and tasted as if half a jar of molasses had been thrown in for good measure; a spoon left in it would probably have stayed upright. While I sipped gingerly away, Uncle George droned on about the various things that had crossed his mind while he was in the kitchen: his sciatica, which was 'aggravating', and the walkers on the beach who wouldn't clear up after their dogs, and the local Woolworth's, which had just raised the price of their light bulbs by a halfpenny a time. Oh, it's a grand old life down in the English provinces, you know, and I wondered why I'd ever left. By this time the clock had walked round to a quarter to eleven and I figured I ought to be getting back to Charing Cross. First, though, there were one or two other things I wanted to know.

'I expect you keep yourself very busy, Uncle George,' I volunteered, 'what with being the branch secretary and so on?'

Uncle George stopped halfway through a story about a garage owner who was supposed to have swindled him out of two secondhand car tyres and nodded his head.

153

'That's right. Why, getting the subs in is a full-time job in itself. Not to mention sending the returns up to HQ. Captain Annesley-Jones has often said that if it weren't for the work I put in the whole thing'd fall apart. Fall apart,' Uncle George said again, with a surprising fluent movement of his hands, which suggested a castle keep tumbling suddenly into dust.

'And I suppose there are the activities to organize?'

'That's it. You've hit the nail on the head. Why, only last week some of us went on the bus to a rally at Margate. Would have cost ninepence each at the usual rate, but I got on to the manager and fixed up a group discount. Thirteen bob for the lot. It's little things like that which make a difference.' He was getting quite animated now, like some half-moribund dog that's just had an ampoule of adrenalin injected into its backside at the vet's. 'And then there's the undesirable activities committee,' Uncle George said.

'What's that when it's at home?'

'Well, you won't find anything about it in the handbook, that's for sure. Captain Annesley-Jones'd have a fit if anyone found out about it.'

'But what does it do?'

'That depends. *Morals*, mostly. Let's say there's a chemist in a decent, respectable street selling French letters. Horrible, dirty things. Well, one day he might find a note pushed through his door. Just friendly, like. And the next week, if he's still selling them, he might find a brick through his window. You see the sort of thing I'm getting at?'

'Absolutely, Uncle George.'

What really struck me in the course of this

recitation, by the way, wasn't so much the thought of all these young chaps in black shirts with faces like fox terriers chucking bricks through chemists' windows—and plainly getting no end of a kick out of it—as the look on Uncle George's mug, which was kind of goofy and mock-stern and bright-eyed all at the same time. You could see he thought he was no end of a fellow for getting mixed up in all this.

I'd drunk almost two-thirds of the tea by now—enough to give the impression that I'd finished it—so I got to my feet.

'I think I'd better be going now, Uncle George. Thanks for the tea.'

Uncle George looked a bit torn, as if he couldn't quite decide if he wanted to see me gone or wanted to prose on some more about the chemists' windows that all his BUF boys were so gaily smashing in. Finally he said: 'That's a pity. We might have had a good old chat.'

'Will Elsie be back soon?' I asked brightly.

'Shouldn't think so,' Uncle George said, in a bit too much of a hurry to be convincing. 'Takes a long time with the shopping does Elsie. A very methodical woman, she is.'

As I lingered in the doorway he said: 'Of course, we're still sorting ourselves out here. Deciding where to put stuff. You might tell your mother that, next time you write to her.'

'I'll make a point of it,' I told him. The Old Lady would be getting full particulars, no question.

Outside the rain had stopped and a weak sun was shining through the clouds, which made 16 Beesley Street look even shabbier than before. Just at that moment a rag-and-bone man took it into his head to trundle past in his cart, and the sound of his cracked bell and the dismal clip-clop of the horse's hoofs was so depressing that you wondered why the inhabitants of Beesley Street didn't all put their heads in the gas oven on the spot. There's no optimism about these days, you know. The old certainties have gone, if they ever existed, and the jobs have gone with them, and if my old English master, Mr Syonsby, had known what had happened to some of the boys he taught he'd be turning in his grave. The rag-and-bone man was so old that he looked as if he'd been exhumed—a little old chap in a threadbare overcoat and a bowler hat tilted to the back of his head. I took a squint into the back of the cart as he pulled up at the roadside and there was nothing in it except a pile of blankets and an enormous chamber pot.

Then, just as I was about head back into the centre of town—there was a train at half eleven I reckoned might do—something else happened. A fat, vague-looking woman with oversized feet that bulged out of her shoes like cottage loaves and a scarf tied over her head came wandering up the street, as if she knew where she was going to but was in two minds about making the effort. I didn't bother to see where she fetched up, for there wasn't the least doubt in my mind as to who she might be. It was Elsie, come back from shopping to bring her winsome presence to her husband's hearth.

*　　　*　　　*

Back at Ramsgate station all the platforms seemed to be coated with pigeon dung and there was a hell of a wind coming in off the sea. The 11.30 was pretty much deserted, apart from what looked like the members of the local WI going up to town to take in a matinée, but in one of the furthermost carriages, head lowered above a copy of *Film Fun* and one hand reaching into a packet of digestive biscuits, who should I find myself walking past but Florence.

'I'd have thought you'd be long gone by now.'

'A girl likes her breakfast,' Florence said. 'Besides, there's a manicurist in the hotel foyer and I wanted to get my cuticles done. I told them to send the bill up to Mr Kilmarnock.' She seemed pleased to see me and patted the seat next to her like an old lady in a café who's promised her wire terrier a special treat with the sugar lumps.

'Looks as if you're well onto your second one,' I volunteered—there was half an Eccles cake next to the biscuit packet, not to mention the wrappers from half a dozen boiled sweets.

'Ah well, there's no telling when lunch might be, is there,' Florence said. 'I got Mr Kilmarnock to pay me in advance, you know.'

'Sound move,' I said, wishing I'd been half as clever. 'Tell me about your friend Gladys.'

'Why d'you want to know?'

'Just interested. What about that club she works at?'

There was definitely something larval about Florence as she sank back into the red plush of the seat, with the sweet wrappers rustling in her lap and the scent of glucose hanging in the air, like a giant grub nestled down on its bed of wood shavings. As there wasn't a great deal of space left beside her, I decided to take the seat opposite.

'I don't know,' she said. 'It's that one at the end

157

of Brewer Street next to the end of the cinema. I can't remember the name.'

This was a bit of a facer, as the only club at the end of Brewer Street next to the cinema was the Debonair, which wasn't much more than a knocking shop.

'Go out with her much, do you?'

'Now and again. Sometimes,' Florence said, leaning towards me across the table with the air of one who imparts some absolutely confidential secret, 'we go and have tea together in Fortnum & Mason.'

'Is that right?'

'Yes. And one time, just when we were finishing the bottom of the pot, do you know what she said to me?'

'No.'

'She said: "Come on Flo, let's have a laugh and get out of here." And do you know we upped and went out of that door double quick past the waitresses and the commissionaire and all without paying and nobody so much as looked in our direction?' She put out a fat hand and gave my wrist a little pat. 'I expect you just fancy her, isn't that right?'

'Who said anything about fancying her?'

'Can always tell, dear.' It was the way she said 'dear' that convinced me she really was a tart. 'But if I was you I'd find better fish to fry. Terrible time she gives men, you know. Why, anyone'd think she didn't really like them at all. Awful, the way she carries on sometimes. Why, there was one young chap nearly threw himself out of an upstairs window on account of her. Right in the middle of Old Compton Street in broad daylight with a hearse

158

going by underneath and a policemen shouting up at him not to be such a fool.'

Well, that was all good to know. Outside there was rain streaking against the window and flocks of crows rising from the distant fields. Slowly, yet purposefully, as if its air of mournful gravity were the only thing that could mock the frivolous conversation taking place inside it, the train pulled on towards Charing Cross.

10

THE LOST WEEKEND

Down at the Berwick Street market
The bananas are eightpence a bunch
The rabbit that lies on the ice-tray
Will do for somebody's lunch.

James Ross, Soho Eclogues

By the time she woke up it was past ten o'clock and there was pale yellow light coming through the gap in the curtain, and the gardenia she had left on the bedside table without putting into water had withered away. As well as the gardenia there was a swizzle stick and a match-clip with the name of a club she did not remember ever having been into. She lay there for a while with one eye buried in the fold of the pillow and the other staring at the swizzle stick and the match-clip, wondering if it was worth trying to go back to sleep, but a mechanical drill had started up in the street outside and in the further distance there was the sound of a man playing the accordion, so in the end she gave it up as a bad job. Sometimes Saturday mornings were the best times, but sometimes not.

There was some Alka-Seltzer in a packet in the cupboard and she mixed it into a tumbler of water while listening to the radio, where John McCormack, or someone who sounded like him, was singing about the *sarn declining*. Sometimes she liked John McCormack and sometimes she liked the man who sang about the little old lady passing by, and sometimes she liked Flanagan and Allen, but on this particular morning she felt that she didn't like anyone at all. By this time the Alka-Seltzer was beginning to have a positive effect, and she sat in the armchair with the least frayed seat with a cup of tea on her lap and revisited the events of the previous night. Then, when this occupation failed her, she thought about the year she had spent living with the girls in the hostel in Kensington and the parties they used to have. Those had, in fact, been the days.

The flat was quite small, but not bad in the mornings when the electric light was turned off and it was possible to ignore the piles of newspapers and the stain on the carpet where someone had dropped the bottle of red wine. At other times it did not pay to look too closely at the surfaces. While she drank the tea she tried to remember any engagements she might have contracted on the previous evening and then forgotten about, and thought she might have agreed to go out with Ian in his car. Then again, she thought that she might have agreed to go and see the people at Surbiton. She had long, pale fingers, which rattled against the teacup while she considered the relative merits of Ian and the people at Surbiton. Looking at the clock on the table she discovered that it was already a quarter to eleven, and this made her feel that she ought to be more decisive in her life. There were girls at the club who took correspondence courses and talked about accompanying rich men on cruises around the Far East, and although she did not want to take correspondence courses or accompany rich men on cruises around the Far East she admired the girls who did these things for their enterprise. She knew that some of them were wrong to cultivate these ideals, but at the same time she could not stop herself admiring them.

Another thing about the flat, apart from its smallness, was how long the bath took to fill up, so she sat on the edge in her dressing gown, trailing her fingers in the water until it was about two-thirds full. While she did this she thought about how much money she would need for the weekend and what, if anything, there might be in the cash box on the bedside table. She could not remember if she had spent the five shillings and twopence that had been there or used it to pay off some of the rent, or whether in fact she had been wholly mistaken about the amount and there was either a great deal more or a great deal less. As she lay in the bath, which was not quite hot enough to cheer her up, but not quite cold enough to depress her, the five shillings and twopence continued to annoy her, so that in the end she had to get out prematurely, put a towel round her waist and rout out the cash box from it hiding place under a chiffon scarf and a box that had once contained bars of Caley's Marching Chocolate. In fact there was thirteen shillings and threepence, and this seemed such an unprecedentedly large sum of money that she spent several minutes working out how it might have got there without coming to any firm conclusion.

It occurred to her that with thirteen shillings and threepence in her handbag she need neither go out with Ian in his car or go and see the people at Surbiton, but the luxury of this choice was not one she was prepared to allow herself. There were footsteps outside on the stairs and she wondered if it might be the postman, only the postman never left anything for her except a letter from her mother, always forwarded on from several other addresses, or a bill or a circular about the babies in Africa. The footsteps went away again, and she sat in a chair once more and read an article in the newspaper about a man who wanted to start a society to stop girls shingling their hair, which he said was bad for the nation's morale.

Presently there was a knock at the door, and going to answer it she found Ian standing on the outside mat. 'I say,' he said, giving no hint as to whether or not he approved of girls answering the door in their dressing gowns, 'but you said you'd be there at eleven.' He was a big blond man with a red face and a moustache, who had been in the Royal Flying Corps during the war and photographed very badly.

'Did I?' she said. 'I was just having a bath. I'm most terribly sorry.'

'Well, I've got the car in Brewer Street,' he said. 'Nicely tuned up and everything and the mag all fixed. I'd thought we'd go down to Worthing.'

'I'll just go and put on some clothes,' she said, wondering what there was to do at Worthing, and he sat on one of the chairs and read the copy of the *Sketch*, while she went to the bedroom and dressed herself in the kind of costume that the magazines she read would have said was neither too chicly ostentatious nor too deliberately low-key.

There was bright sun shining as they came out into the street, and the clouds had receded, and he said: 'Looks as if it's going to be a nice day,' and she said, quite earnestly, 'It does, doesn't it?' 'The car's just this way,' he explained, and she thought of all

163

the other men she had been out in motor cars with, in Kent, Sussex and the destinations even further afield, and how the wind got into her hair and it was always too noisy to talk to the person you were driving with. The car was a sports model and had at some point in its recent history collided with a large, immoveable object. Its incidental attractions included a suitcase, which had been jammed into the jockey seat, a pair of wash-leather motoring gloves and a road atlas which had 'Property of Holborn & St Pancras Public Library' stamped on its cover.

They moved off by degrees. 'Of course,' he said, 'we may not get to Worthing, but I think it's important to have an end in mind, don't you?'

'I think you're absolutely right,' she said.

He had an office somewhere in Chiswick and sometimes composed the letterpress for toothpaste advertisements. They proceeded down Whitehall, where the sentries stood guard in their boxes, past the Cenotaph, where there was already scaffolding being erected for the parade, and over the river into the mean little streets beyond, and she thought about men, and their moustaches, and the things they sometimes said about Ramsay Macdonald and the National Government, or the traffic signals on the Great West Road, or the best place to go in St John's Wood for a decent supper for five shillings a head.

'I say,' he said, 'are you feeling all right?'

'Actually,' she said, 'I have the most awful headache.'

'I'm not feeling too wonderful myself,' he said. 'Late night and all that. What say we stop for a quick one?'

'Yes,' she said. 'I think that would be a very wise idea,' and so they stopped at a roadhouse just outside Croydon where there were half a dozen other cars drawn up in a semicircle on the asphalt car park and a beer garden with a couple of decayed benches and some children's toys thrown in a heap. Inside there was a smell of smoke, and a fat woman in a pink dress and an apron was unloading plates of fish and chips from the service hatch.

'What'll you have?' he asked.

'Oh, I don't know,' she said. There were more plates appearing out of the serving hatch now: steak and kidney pie and sausage and mash. The sight of them made her feel sick. 'Perhaps I shan't have anything,' she said.

'Nonsense,' he told her. The hair of his eyebrows was so blond that it was as if they had been shaved. 'Double doubles. That's the only thing to drink at a time like this.'

After they had drunk the double doubles they felt slightly better and ordered up sandwiches from the bar, and got into conversation with some people who were driving down to Hove to attend an antiques fair and said that they had once had dinner in the same restaurant as Max Miller. When they got outside the sky was darkening and the rain had come on again: the Surrey pine trees danced in the wind.

'Do you know,' he said, 'I never really wanted to go to Worthing in the first place?'

'Didn't you?' she said. She was still thinking about the people who had once had supper with Max Miller. 'Why not?'

'I don't know. It's rather far. Let's go to East

165

Grinstead instead.'

'What is there at East Grinstead?'

'I don't know. It's supposed to be rather a decent place. Why don't we go there?'

'All right then,' she said. 'Let's go there.'

And so they went to East Grinstead, which did not, she thought, seem so very interesting, and where, additionally, it was raining quite hard. They ate slices of Fuller's Walnut Cake in a teashop and looked out of the window at a British Legion parade that was going past, and which they found so intensely funny for some reason that they laughed out loud and were stared at disapprovingly by the other tea-drinkers, and she wondered if this was the sixth time she had come out with Ian in his car or the seventh, and whether life offered more exciting prospects that she had not yet found out about, or if Ian and his car and the East Grinstead teashop were the limit of experience, beyond which no more satisfying arrangement could ever be obtained. There were times when she wanted to be a mannequin and go to the sort of parties that were described in the *Bystander*, and there were times when she wanted to sit in the drawing room of a house of the kind that her sister had once lived in at Guildford reading *If Winter Comes*, but these occasions never coincided with an opportunity to put them into practice.

When they came out after tea the light was fading over the Downs and, as there was a cinema on the other side of the street, they walked across to it and saw *Convention City* with Joan Blondell and Guy Kibbee. Twenty minutes after the film started he fell asleep and she sat staring into the darkness, wondering how things had turned out this way and why she was sitting in a cinema in East Grinstead on a Saturday afternoon with a man whose eyebrows looked as if they had been shaved off and who almost certainly had a wife waiting for him in Putney. And then, because Joan Blondell was so funny and everyone said the film had been criticized by the League of Decency, she cheered up and began to pay attention, so that even the sound of his snoring was not quite the discomfort it might have been.

'Well, that was fun wasn't it?' he said when they stood outside in the street again, where it was properly dark and the shutters were up across the shopfronts, and she nodded her head and said, yes, it was fun. 'And now what we need is a good stiff drink,' he went on, and she nodded her head again and said, yes, that was exactly what they did need.

And so they went into the pub next to the cinema, which was empty except for a man with a strawberry-coloured birthmark on his face and a bulldog he said he was trying to sell, and some boys who had just come back from playing rugger and talked soberly about how the Number Eight would never play for Sussex if he trained every day for a year, and had some brandy cocktails.

'The question,' Ian said seriously, 'is whether we stay here or push on somewhere else.'

'Actually,' she said, 'I should quite like to be getting back, as I've got my friend Annie to see, you know.' She wondered if he knew that her friend Annie was an invention.

'That's all right,' he said. 'I wouldn't want you to miss seeing your friend Annie. But look here, we must have another one, you know, before we set off.' And so they had another brandy cocktail and got talking to a man who had just come in who told them that he had been at Vimy Ridge. And Ian said that he had been at Vimy Ridge, or rather not at it, but had flown over it in a Harry Tate. And the man said that it was people like him who had won the war, and they ought to have another drink.

While the man was getting the drinks she saw on the clock that it was half past seven. 'Really, you know,' she said, 'I must be getting back to see my friend Annie.'

'That's right,' he said. There was a football special on the table and he was reading the results. 'But it would be rude not to have a drink with this chap who was at Vimy Ridge when I flew over it in a Harry Tate, wouldn't it?' And she said, yes, she supposed it would. She thought that, if it came to it, she could go the railway station and take the train back to London, but then she remembered that she had forgotten the thirteen shillings and threepence and that there were only a couple of sixpences in her purse. They had stopped drinking brandy cocktails and were drinking gin and its, which Ian said were just the thing for an autumn night and wouldn't give you a head if you drank a gallon of them, and she thought—the feeling had been going on for a while—that if she didn't have something to eat she would very likely faint. 'Please,' she said, as the second round of gin and its was brought over— it was Ian's turn now to treat the man who had fought at Vimy Ridge—'do you think I could have a sandwich or something?'

'Well, if you're hungry,' Ian said, 'then we really ought to have something to eat. Isn't that right?'

And so ten minutes later she found herself sitting in the dining room attached to the pub while

Ian ordered them sardines on toast followed by steak and kidney pie. 'I did tell Annie,' she said, 'that I'd be there by nine,' and Ian, who was busy tasting the Chianti to see if it was corked, which he said was always a danger in these country pubs, nodded his head and said that if they left by 8.15 they could be home by nine or so, and surely Annie wouldn't mind that, and if she did he personally would explain to her that it was all his fault, and wouldn't that do? And she nodded her head—the sardines had come now, and she was feeling slightly better—and said that, yes, she supposed it would. The man who had been at Vimy Ridge, and had mysteriously attached himself to them, said that he had something to say, and when they asked what it was he said that it was a confession, and that he had never fought in the war at all, and that he had been graded C3 on account of his flat feet and had to work on the land instead. And Ian said that he needn't mind and there were plenty of people who did fight in the war who were more of a hindrance than a help, and the man who hadn't been at Vimy Ridge said that he was a gentleman, and that he ought to live at East Grinstead as it was the most dead-alive place and needed cheering up.

By now it was a quarter to nine and when they had finished the meal and gone back into the bar she gave a little tug at Ian's sleeve and showed him the clock. 'Yes, I know, Annie,' he said, and went on talking to the man who hadn't fought at Vimy Ridge about how difficult Harry Tates were to get off the ground and how they had always ended up ploughing through hedges and other obstructions and it was a wonder how any bombs were ever dropped by them at all.

She had just made up her mind that she was going to get up and ask him to lend her the money for the railway fare when some Salvation Army people came into the pub selling the *War Cry*, and of course they had to give them a round of applause and ask them if they wanted anything.

'I promise you,' Ian said, when she showed signs of being tired of the man who hadn't been at Vimy Ridge, and was now telling them about his motor-bicycle, 'that just as soon as I've had this drink we'll go. Now, will that do?' And she nodded her head and said that she supposed it would.

Great stretches of time seemed to pass. The pub was filling up now, with middle-aged men in bowler hats and girls and their young men, and inscrutable old ladies with gigantic handbags who ordered gin and peppermint, and the noise became unbearable. The man who hadn't been at Vimy Ridge took Ian off to speak to some friends of his at the other side of the bar and when he came back she saw, to her horror, that it was nearly twenty to ten. 'No point in going back at this time of night,' Ian said. 'We'll just have to take a room here. Will that be all right?' And she nodded her head and said that she supposed it would.

And so they went to the reception desk beyond the bar and ordered the room, and Ian signed their names, *Mr and Mrs I. C. G. Alloway*, in the visitors' book. 'No use crying over spilt milk, is there?' Ian said after they had done this, and she nodded her head and said, no, she supposed there wasn't any point. 'But what I really feel like,' Ian said, as if they had been discussing this particular point for the past half-hour, 'is some mulled ale.' And so the barman drew him off a pint of beer and someone took the poker out of the fire and plunged it in so that the steam boiled up, and Ian drank it off and wiped his forehead, which was redder than ever, and said that that was a tonic for the troops and no mistake.

There were some people there who had just come back from Kenya, and Ian said was it nice out there and were the blacks kept properly in their places, and the people who had just come back from Kenya said that it was and they were, and Ian said that was something to be thankful for. The barmaid was calling 'Time!' and 'Time, ladies and gentleman please!' and the people who had just come back from Kenya were all for them coming back to their place and having coffee, but she told Ian that she had such a head she would scream if she had to stay up any longer, and so they went upstairs as the landlord locked up the front door and the barman went round tipping ashtrays into an upturned dustbin lid. There was a terrible amount of smoke in the air and everything smelled of beer and gin and sawdust.

The bedroom was on the small side and had no fire and the first thing Ian did was to fall onto the double bed and go to sleep on it. At first this struck her as highly amusing, but then she realized that, like the room, the double bed was on the small side, and that if she couldn't persuade him to move she would have to find somewhere else to sleep. Outside there was a flurry of wings in the dark and an owl came up close the window and then went away again. She pushed him once or twice and said, 'Ian,' and 'Ian, wake up,' several times in his ear, but it was no good. Curiously, she was quite wideawake now. She looked round the room for something to interest her, but there was only a copy of *John Bull* and a book about flowering annuals. Somewhere in the distance a clock was striking the quarter. She said, '*Ian*,' again into his ear, so loudly that it was almost a shout, but got no response. There were some extra blankets underneath the bed, and an old counterpane that smelled of mothballs, and so she pulled them out and wrapped them round herself and sat in the armchair by the window, thinking about the hostel in Kensington and the parties they'd had there, and a young man who said he was going to be a Liberal MP, but everyone else said would end up as a pawnbroker, until eventually, towards morning, she fell asleep.

*   *   *

When she woke up the church clock had just begun to strike ten and there was a pain in her shoulder from where it had rested on the chair-back. Ian was still fast asleep face down on the bed, but when she went across and said, 'Ian,' quite loudly in his ear he came suddenly awake and asked, 'I say, was I asleep?' And she said, 'Yes you were, rather.' There was a terrible pain in her head to add to the one in her shoulder, and she looked in her handbag to see if there were any aspirin, but the packet was quite empty.

It was an annoying habit of Ian's that, however much he had had to drink the previous night, he always felt perfectly all right the next morning. Sitting up on the mattress, with one hand held out to brace himself, he said: 'Well, that was rather an evening, wasn't it?' And she said, 'Yes, I suppose it was rather an evening in a way.'

172

'I daresay we'd better see if we can find some breakfast,' he said, and she said, yes, she supposed they ought to.

Halfway down the staircase they came upon a girl polishing the banisters, and she gathered from the look the girl gave her that she didn't think she was Ian's wife. 'I do wish that people wouldn't look at one like that,' she said quite loudly as they descended, and Ian said, yes, he wished so too. His face was dead white, like a piece of cold boiled veal, and it seemed as if he had no eyebrows at all.

The dining room was quite empty, with only a few places set, but Ian went into the kitchen and routed out the publican's wife, who promised to get them something to eat.

'Shocking bad service you get at places like this,' Ian said affably. He had lit a cigarette, and the smoke curled mysteriously around the corners of his face and his sparse, sandy hair. He was forty-one, and a bit old for this kind of thing.

'What are they going to bring us?' she asked, and he said: 'Oh, bacon, sausage, toast, that kind of thing I expect.' And she thought that if there were fried eggs she would be sick, because of all things, when one wakes up with a headache, a fried egg is the most disgusting.

Happily there were no fried eggs, so she ate some pieces of toast and drank three cups of tea in quick succession and felt better. Ian was reading the *News of the World*, which someone had left on chair nearby, where the front page stories were all about a white-slaving operation which the police said they had broken up in Blackpool and a party where somebody's hunter had galloped up the front stairs and had to be rescued by a winch.

Outside the window of the dining room was a wide street with a brick wall behind it where girls in Sunday dresses and their best coats could be seen bicycling to church.

She said: 'Can we go back to London, please? There are things I really have to do.'

'Certainly,' he said, with an immense solicitousness. 'As a matter of fact I've a lot on myself, you know.'

When they had finished breakfast they went and had coffee in the main part of the pub and talked to the landlord, who was emptying the spittoons from the previous night and making desultory attempts to polish the horse brasses.

'Nice little crib you've got here,' Ian said—the colour was coming back into his face now, and it looked less like a piece of cold boiled veal—and the landlord said, yes, it was a nice little crib, although you got all sorts coming in these days, and nothing had ever been the same since the war.

Outside the bicycling girls had all gone, and been replaced by a file of Boy Scouts marching to church parade and some evil-looking old men who knocked over the piles of leaves with their walking sticks.

By the time they had finished their coffee and admired the horse brasses, which the landlord insisted on showing them, it was a quarter to twelve.

'Are you all right?' Ian asked as they walked out into the street to find the car. 'Only you look rather pale, you know.'

'No, I'm perfectly all right,' she said. Her head had stopped aching, but there was still a pain in her shoulder from where the chair-back had pressed against it.

It had rained overnight and the streets of East Grinstead looked grey and menacing. There was a Wesleyan chapel nearby and they could hear the sound of a hymn being sung in gruff, plebeian voices. After a bit they found the car and drove off through the Sussex forests, along tiny lanes thick with bracken, from which startled pheasants occasionally took flight.

'Do you know,' he said, 'what I should really like, above all things, is the hair of the dog that bit me?'

'I really must be getting back,' she said.

'Of course you do,' he said. 'I understand that perfectly. But you do look terribly pale, you know.'

'I really do have to be getting back,' she said, a bit less confidently, and so they stopped at a pub on the London Road, where some people in ancient cars had come to rest on the way back from an excursion to Brighton.

'Double doubles,' Ian said, coming back from the bar with a tumbler in each hand. 'It's the only way, you know, at a time like this.' And so she drank the double double, or most of it, and ate some potato chips out of a bag, and thought about the hostel at Kensington, and the woman who ran it, Mrs Bellerby, and how she sat by the radiogram every night cable-stitching a jersey for her niece. The pub did not serve hot food at lunch-time, but Ian said that a pork pie and a sandwich would suit him perfectly.

In this way another great stretch of time passed, and she had the odd sensation that all the heads of the people in the pub, talking and shouting to each other, had turned into a single monstrous head screaming and screaming at her so that she wanted to run away from it.

'I really do have to be getting back,' she said, almost bursting into tears as she did so.

They drove off onto the London Road, where there were lorries sailing past and an Armstrong-Siddeley had broken down, which an RAC man was staring at glumly.

'Always something depressing about a Sunday afternoon, isn't there?' Ian said, and she nodded her head and said, yes, she supposed there was.

As they came into the outskirts of London the light began to fade and she was struck by the rows of dreadful little houses stretching away from them on every side, the Purley villas and the neat little Croydon semis and the Clapham slums. There was mist over the plinths in Trafalgar Square.

He dropped her on the corner of Wardour Street and she stood and watched the car drive off and then let herself into the house and climbed up the staircase to her flat, where there was a musty smell and the curtains were still drawn from the day before. In her absence a note had been pushed through the letter box by the old lady downstairs. It said: *Dear Miss —— I am afraid that the noise you made when returning home on Friday night was quite unacceptable, and I fear I shall have to refer the matter to the landlord . . .* Once she had finished reading it she opened a tin of salmon and fed it to herself absent-mindedly with a teaspoon. After this she lay down on the bed and went to sleep. It was about half past five, and quite quiet for the time of day.

11

HOPING AND WAITING

Let's go down to Trafalgar Square
And on to Buckingham Palace
The guardsmen are out in Victoria Street
But no one's marrying Alice

James Ross, Soho Eclogues

'Quiet night was it yesterday?'

'Mm-hm. Not so bad. A couple of drunks got in and tried to make the croupier get up a hand of three-card brag, but Edgar soon put them out.'

'It could have been worse then?'

'That's right. It could have been worse.'

It was a week after the trip to Ramsgate and I was sitting in Sammy's office at the Toreador. It was about eleven o'clock in the morning and outside in Dean Street there was a nurse selling poppies from a tray, while an enormously fat man and a teenage boy with a cast in one eye tried to shift a piano through the double doors of the Cadenza.

'Tell you what, though,' Sammy said. He was in one of his confidential moods, and had already told me that his wife had burned the toast that morning and had raised one hell of a stink about a lace-edged handkerchief that had fallen out of the jacket pocket of his best suit before it went off to the cleaner's. 'That chap Rafferty was round again yesterday.'

Usually I perked up no end when Sammy

mentioned Mr Rafferty, who owned the Castlereagh in Lexington Street, and sometimes came round to ask him if he wanted to sell the club, as Sammy did a very good impression of him eating an olive off a cocktail stick. But this particular morning I was so browned off that I barely listened. Eve's darts again, as Captain Tanqueray used to say whenever one of the postal clerks looked especially green around the gills, because in the time since I came back from Ramsgate I hadn't so much as set eyes on Gladys. I'd called round at the flat a couple of times and she hadn't been there, and then a note had come to Rathbone Place asking me to meet her in a pub in Hanway Street, but she'd never shown. I'd hung about in Meard Street once to see if I could catch her coming back, but there was nothing doing. To all intents and purposes she'd vanished off the face of the earth.

To make matters worse, Gladys wasn't the only thing worrying me. I'd been back to the Black House a couple more times, and further ingratiated myself with Baxter, but there was no sign of the character who'd waded in with the knuckleduster in the King's Road. I hadn't got any further with the chap who lived in the ground-floor room at Rathbone Place either. So, as you can see, I was in a pretty miserable state, listening to Sammy tell me about Mr Rafferty's latest offer—he always made Sammy the same offer and Sammy always turned him down—and not even the sound of the piano crashing over on its side and the sulky redhead (properly dressed this time) running out to give the fat bloke and his assistant an earful could push away that sinking feeling you have when you can't do anything about the jam you're in because the people who could help you in one way or another have simply disappeared.

'And while we're at it,' Sammy said, 'I need to have a word with you about the rents.'

'Nothing wrong is there?' I asked. I'd been doing a pretty good job just lately, as far as I recollected, apart from the hopeless cases, which Sammy and I both knew it would take a bailiff to shift.

'No, nothing wrong,' Sammy said. He had the ledger out on his desk and was running a forefinger up and down the columns. 'Be good if you could do something about that house in Meard Street, though.'

'Would it?' No point in asking which house in Meard Street he meant, of course.

'That's right. Ma Wisbeach going on about her window frames I can just about put up with, but here's Sibierski not paid a bean in six weeks, and that Miss Marlborough isn't what you'd call reliable.'

'Never seems to be anyone at home,' I said, a bit defensively.

'I know, I know,' Sammy said. He sounded even more Jewish when he was irritated. 'As for that Miss Marlborough, you should hear some of the stories Lennie used to tell about her.' They'd got the piano upright again by now and the fat man was smoking a fag and looking mournfully up and down the street like a greyhound owner whose dog has gone arse over tip coming out of the slips. 'Look, why don't you go round there again now and see what's up? Leave a note on the door, if necessary.'

'Good idea,' I said, rather glad of another excuse to see if I could get to talk to Gladys, and a bit fearful, too, of what she might or mightn't say to me when I did get to see her. That's the trouble with those sulky girls, you see. Half the time, when they look as if they want to chew your head off, you don't especially want them to talk to you, and the other half of the time, when they're graciously disposed to be civil, you can't think of anything to say in return. The solution, I suppose, is not to fall for sulky girls, but that's a trick I've never got round to learning.

*   *   *

Outside in Dean Street someone had left a trail of cauliflower stalks all over the pavement together with a pile of tracts with a flaring headline that read: SINNERS BEWARE, FOR CHRIST RETURNS WITH A FLAMING SWORD. You get some queer stuff lying around the place in Soho. There was a paper shop three doors down, and I thought I'd go and see whether the new *Crucible* was in and, if so, whether Mortimer-Smith had printed a poem of mine that had been standing over for the past three months. In normal circumstances I'd have contrived to browse through the literary pages and see if the poem was there without having to pay for it, but the newsagent was one of those vigilant, interfering types and I virtually had to stick a tanner down on the counter before I was allowed to pick it up. Anyway, there was no sign of the poem. What there certainly was, on the other hand, was Professor Battycharya's article about Madame Blavatsky, all seventeen pages of it, and a signed leader by Chalkie canvassing the need for a 'new moral seriousness', whatever that was. I was still wondering what had got into Chalkie, and what

Mortimer-Smith intended to do about it, when I came up the stairs at Meard Street and discovered Mrs Wisbeach and a coloured chap whose face looked vaguely familiar in conference on the landing.

'Good morning, Mr Ross,' Mrs Wisbeach said, looking a bit like the headmistress of Cavendish Grange when Matilda has been found smoking in the boiler room. 'You will remember Mr Laal?'

The last time I'd seen Mr Laal he'd been sprawling on the carpet in the company of a hank of butter-muslin, but clearly no one needed reminding of this.

'Delighted to see you again,' I said heartily, and Mr Laal gave a sheepish grin, like Duleepsinhji cutting to leg, and fairly scuttled off down the staircase as Mrs Wisbeach and I watched him go.

I was just about to carry on up the stairs—after all, Mrs Wisbeach's rent was paid up on the nail—when she gave me a conspiratorial look and said: 'Perhaps, Mr Ross, you would care to have a cup of tea?'

'I certainly should, Mrs Wisbeach.' A pot of Pekoe Points is a pot of Pekoe Points, after all. Besides, there might be some news about Gladys. So I followed her into the flat, where there was another wall of tinned beetroot drawn up on the kitchen table and Hercules was chewing up a copy of the day before's *Morning Post*. Remembering my calf, which was still on the sore side, it was all I could do to stop kicking him.

'Down, Hercules, down,' Mrs Wisbeach said absent-mindedly before turning to face me above the beetroot. 'You may be wondering, Mr Ross, why it is that I should be entertaining Mr Laal on these

181

premises?'

I couldn't for the life of me see what it had to do with yours truly. On the other hand, it struck me that Mrs Wisbeach was looking for a bit of sympathy, so I said rousingly: 'I must say that the thought had occurred to me, Mrs Wisbeach.'

'The fact is, Mr Ross, that Mr Laal has provided me with a full explanation of the events which both of us witnessed.' There was a pause. In the background I could hear Hercules slobbering over the *Morning Post*. 'An explanation which, I am pleased to say, exonerates him entirely from the suspicion under which he was placed.'

I wasn't quite sure what this meant. Had someone fixed the whole business? Faked the voice? Planted the butter-muslin in Mr Laal's jacket pocket? I was about to ask one of these questions, but Mrs Wisbeach put a finger melodramatically to her lips.

'Not a word more, Mr Ross. I have gravely impugned the character of a fellow-seeker after truth, and it is up to me to make amends.'

Well, that was one way of looking at it, I suppose. The tea had brewed by now, and we repaired to the sitting room to drink it. Oddly enough the planchette was out on the table again. When Mrs Wisbeach saw that I'd seen it she gave a little laugh.

'Mr Laal has been helping me with certain— ah—*investigations*, which, between you and me, Mr Ross, I should prefer to go no further than this room.'

As far as I was concerned, Mrs Wisbeach and Mr Laal could sacrifice a goat in the fireplace and summon up Cronos himself from the coal scuttle if they had a mind, but I knew what was expected of me so I smiled gallantly and said: 'Your secret is safe with me, Mrs Wisbeach.'

'Your discretion is very much appreciated, Mr Ross.' There was still something worrying her, I could see. After a minute or so's silence, while I was halfway through the next cup of Pekoe Points, she said suddenly: 'I don't mind telling you, Mr Ross, that I have had the most curious experience with Miss Marlborough.'

'In what way curious, Mrs Wisbeach?'

'Well, it was the afternoon on which she very kindly agreed to look after Hercules. He gets very lonely while I'm away, you see, and of course there are occasions when he needs to be . . . well, to be taken outside. But when I came back— you will hardly credit this, but there it is—Miss Marlborough seemed to have shut him up in the broom cupboard.'

It's the listener's job to act as Little Sir Echo on these occasions, so I instantly piped up: 'In the broom cupboard, Mrs Wisbeach?'

'That's right. In the broom cupboard. When I demanded an explanation, she said that he had been chasing a mouse and the door had become stuck. Did you ever hear such a rigmarole? What *can* she have been thinking of?'

'I'm sure I don't know, Mrs Wisbeach.' Then a thought occurred to me. 'Have you seen her recently?'

'Miss Marlborough? No, I have not. Although I am afraid I had to write her a letter of complaint at the weekend. The noise that young woman makes when she comes home! And at such *obscure times*, too.'

'It's my belief, Mrs Wisbeach, that Miss

Marlborough suffers very badly from nerves.'

Usually when you offer this excuse to elderly ladies it gets shot down like a grouse over the North York moors, but Mrs Wisbeach only nodded her head.

'Does she, do you think? How very interesting. Well, of course, if that were true it would explain a very great deal.'

'Yes, I suppose it would.'

'Do you know, Mr Ross, if there is one thing I believe I have learned in my life—and my husband used to say it, too, when he was involved in the Red Cross—it is that one must not make assumptions about people.'

'I'm sure you're right, Mrs Wisbeach.' We were getting towards the bottom of the pot now, and I reckoned it was time to leave.

'Take Mr Laal now. It would be so easy, so very easy, to judge him by the colour of his skin, or . . . or by that ridiculous incident that took place the other week, for which, if you don't mind my saying so, Mr Ross, I fear that Mr Warburton must take a great deal of the blame. But really I find him a very sensitive man. Do you know that he took his BA at the University of Calcutta?'

There was no knowing how long this might go on. 'I'm afraid I really must be going, Mrs Wisbeach. Professional responsibilities, you understand.'

'I understand perfectly, Mr Ross. And if you should happen to see her soon, please tell Miss Marlborough that I sympathize *very much* with her afflictions.'

'I shall certainly do that, Mrs Wisbeach,' I assured her. In fact, if it was anything to do with me I intended to see Miss Marlborough within the next half-hour. But the second-floor back, which I reached a short while later, was as empty as the grave, so after banging on the knocker half a dozen times I scribbled a note on the silver paper from a fag packet—*Desperate to see you, hope all well, James*—and pushed it through the letter box. Then, just to demonstrate—to myself, if not to anyone else—that this wasn't wholly a pleasure trip, I went back downstairs and rapped smartly on Sibierski's door. Would you believe? There was nothing doing there either, and there I was out on the pavement in Meard Street again with nothing to show for except the memory of Mrs Wisbeach's Pekoe Points.

By now it was gone twelve, and by rights I should have carried on down Meard and on to Brewer. Somehow, though, I didn't fancy it. I had an idea, you see, that I ought to head off to the Black House again and see what news I could pick up—not just about Mr Knuckleduster, but the whole Soho clean-up business that Uncle George's newsletter had been so cryptic about. So after I'd had a sandwich at the Denmark Arms—one of these days I really would have that slap-up lunch I'd promised myself—I walked down to Piccadilly Circus, bought a *Star* to see if any of the murder cases I was following had got any further, and took a bus down the King's Road. It was getting on into autumn now, and London had that smoky, end-of-year feel which is so delicious, my dear, if you live in a Sussex village but gets on your nerves when it's accompanied by endless fog and the sound of motor horns. The top deck of the bus was full of middle-aged women with cardboard boxes and startling hats who all seemed to know each other and thought that everything they saw out of the window was screamingly funny, and I thought to myself that it was all J. B. Priestley's fault really, and if he hadn't started writing about them then they wouldn't feel they could go about behaving in the way they did.

The King's Road was properly autumnal, with piles of leaves burning in the gardens and well-wrapped-up women saying to each other, 'And then, my dear, he played one no-trump would you believe, and it's such a shame Hermione doesn't see anything in that Ashington boy because his father's just got the Governorship.' The Black House was deathly quiet, which didn't surprise me because there was no pattern to the place. Half the time it was like an ant heap with chaps running in and out as if the revolution was booked for teatime, and the other half it was more or less empty, with charwomen swabbing the tiles and carrying mugs of tea nobody quite knew where, with Baxter wandering up and down the corridors saying, 'Splendid, carry on,' to anyone he thought needed cheering up. Mosley I'd never set eyes on, though the other chaps said he was about the place fairly often. Curiously, the first person I saw when I got through the door was Blennerhassett. He was dressed up in the full rig of black whipcord jodhpurs and a black pullover and looked like an exceptionally keen whippet taking the scent.

'Your annual leave's lasted a long time,' I said, by way of a greeting.

'Oh, I'm not on holiday,' Blennerhassett said with immense seriousness. He had a form in his hand that read *Nightwatch cocoa requisition B/11* and was clearly enjoying himself no end. 'But

186

you see we've a branch in Flood Street and the managing partner sometimes lets me have half an hour extra for lunch. It's surprising what you can do in that time if you set your mind to it.'

Well, Corporal Hackett used to say that in the NCOs' mess on a Saturday night with the chimes striking eleven and four pints of bitter lined up in front of him, but I didn't think Blennerhassett would appreciate the comparison.

'Any sign of Baxter?' I asked.

'I believe Mr Baxter is in the kitchens,' Blennerhassett said, with the faintest perceptible stress on the 'Mr', just to let me know that I'd put up a black. So I went down the back staircase to the part of the building known as the canteen, which consisted of a sink, a gas cooker, a couple of cupboards and a shelf stacked up with enormous tubs of marmalade. Baxter was inspecting some Cornishware mugs that someone had just unpacked out of a box, looked distinctly liverish and didn't seem particularly glad to see me.

'Ah, Ross,' he said. For some reason half the mugs had *A Present to a Good Boy from Lostwithiel* printed on the sides. 'At a loose end, eh?'

'Not really, sir,' I said, coming to attention and contriving to suggest that I was as keen as mustard. 'I've just met Mr Blennerhassett and we're going to sort out some more leaflets in the post room.'

'Splendid,' Baxter said. There was a bit of a silence, but then, presumably as a way of letting me know that all this enthusiasm was appreciated by those in positions of authority, he went on: 'Settling in here are you, Ross?'

'I like to think so, sir.'

'That's the ticket. Uniform coming soon?'

'Having it made up, sir.' The conversation looked as if it might be coming to an end, which wasn't what I had in mind, so I said: 'Quite a business, sir, handing out those leaflets the other week. In fact, if those other chaps hadn't turned up out of the blue I don't know where we should have been.'

'Oh yes,' Baxter said, a touch uneasily. 'Davenport and his chums, wasn't it?'

'Don't know his name, sir.'

'Methods are a bit unorthodox, but we like to have him with us.' There was clearly something else bothering him, over and above the thought of Davenport careening down the King's Road with a knuckleduster. 'I say, Ross, I don't suppose you know anyone with any experience of waiting at table?'

Well, that was an easy one. 'As a matter of fact I have some myself, sir.'

It was the truth as well. During the last month of the war, when they'd given up trying to censor the mail, I'd worked as a mess waiter down at the big camp outside Eastbourne. Rotten job it was, with never a tip in sight and being abused by fat majors over the eyes in the potatoes. Anyway, Baxter positively glowed, like old Bosun McHearty when young Dick Dauntless has just saved the ship from ruin.

'Don't mind my asking where, do you Ross?'

'Southern Command, sir. Nineteen eighteen.'

'Of course! Ex-serviceman, aren't you? Well, the thing is that something rather important has come up.'

'Has it, sir?'

'It certainly has. The whole thing's highly confidential—only just got wind of it myself.' And here Baxter looked a bit crestfallen at being left out of the loop. 'But it seems that Sir Oswald has arranged a private dinner down in the country tomorrow night. The local retainers aren't up to strength and if there's one thing Sir Oswald can't stand it's hired staff, so I've been told—that is, I have undertaken—to supply the extra men myself.'

'What sort of an affair is it, sir?' I asked, thinking that this would be just the sort of thing Haversham would go nuts on.

'Oh, you know, the cause and so forth. But I'm led to believe'—and here Baxter gave an absolutely slavish look—'that there's a very distinguished guest expected.' The way he said 'distinguished' made me think it couldn't be anyone less than Ramsay Mac or the Archbishop of Canterbury. In fact it sounded just the kind of beano it would pay me to eavesdrop on, so I looked very serious and said: 'What time shall I report for duty, sir?'

I think Baxter may actually have patted me on the back for my keenness. Anyhow, he told me to be there sharp at 5.30 the next afternoon, where transport would be provided to ferry me and one or two other likely lads down to the Leader's country pile—it was in Buckinghamshire somewhere—and that I could expect to be brought back to Chelsea at around midnight. I thought I'd go and tell Blennerhassett the good news—after all, he might have wanted to come himself—but one of the other chaps told me he'd gone back to Flood Street, and as there was no one much about and the leaflets in the post room had all been sorted out, I decided I'd sling my hook.

Queerly enough, on the bus going back to Soho I cheered up no end. It was even money the dinner down in the country would turn up something I could use to my advantage. The practical side of it didn't worry me at all, by the way. Anyone can wait at table. You just have to look attentive, say, 'What may I have the pleasure of offering you, sir?' at regular intervals and make sure you don't spill anything. And who knew, maybe the business with Gladys would work out all right. Stranger things had happened.

Anyway, this mood lasted all the way back to Oxford Street, where it had started raining again and some hunger-marchers were grimly processing on their way to Downing Street. They were sad-looking chaps, and the banners they were carrying were all about standing up for justice, but somehow I didn't think we'd see them down at the Black House. I got off the bus in the hunger-marchers' wake and trudged up to Rathbone Place. And then two odd things happened in the space of half a minute. The first was that just inside the front door I bumped into a chap called Witherspoon, who was the only other person I knew at my digs and who I'd once lent an umbrella to—an umbrella, more to the point, that had never come back.

'Sorry about that gamp,' Witherspoon said when he saw me. He was about fifty and a great one for the drink. 'Give it to you now if you like.'

'That's all right,' I said, and then a thought struck me. 'I say,' I went on. 'Don't suppose you know the name of the chap in the ground floor back?' And I pointed at the door with my thumb.

''Smatter of fact I do,' Witherspoon said. 'Cohen, I believe. Don't see him about much, though.'

'Don't see any of us about much,' I lobbed back. Witherspoon looked as if he might jolly soon suggest a trip to the Newman Arms, which was where he spent most of his time, but I shook him off and breezed upstairs to my room. And there, would you credit it, was a letter from Gladys, written in red ink on paper that couldn't have cost less than five bob a packet. It went:

Dear James,

It was such a shame about last week, and I really must apologize. Unfortunately I have been away or I should have written before. You must be horribly cross with me! Anyway, it would be lovely if you could come round one evening. Do drop in if you have a spare hour or so.

Best love,
Gladys

No doubt about it, things were looking up.

12

AN UNEXPECTED GUEST

Princess Bibesco and Mr Bryan Guinness
Were seen at the Embassy Club
In Brewer a chap is swapping two soup-spoons
For a packet of stale ready-rub

James Ross, Soho Eclogues

When it came to it, I might just as well have not bothered to go to bed that night. I've never been the world's greatest shut-eye merchant, but that particular eight-hour stretch was like something out of Dante. At first I tried concentrating on the letter Gladys had sent me, and all the splendid times we were going to have—I'm an optimist about women, you see, despite all the pressing evidence to the contrary—but pretty soon I was fretting myself over all the things that looked as if they might go wrong over the next couple of days. Top of the list was the trip down to Buckinghamshire and the evening with Sir Oswald. God knew what that might involve, but I had a shrewd idea that waiting at table wouldn't be the half of it. Then there was Mr Cohen, whoever he was, and what he'd turn out to be like. Finally there was Gladys herself, who, the more I thought about her, seemed one of the queerest propositions I'd ever come across.

Never mind the expensive get-up, and the not being able to pay your way (which was a combination I'd come across once or twice before, thank you very much) or whatever she'd been up to with Master Davenport, there was still the question of her friend Flo, my companion on the voyage to Ramsgate, who so far as I could judge, if not actually a tart, was only one step away from it. It's my experience, you see, that nice girls don't hang about with tarts, however much they may sympathize with them, because, when it comes down to it, you don't want oily little chaps in bowler hats petitioning you in the street. Perhaps, on the other hand, there was a side to Gladys that was all heart-felt compassion and there-but-for-the grace-of-God-goeth-I, but all I could say was that I'd seen precious few examples of it. Anyway, all this was enough to put me in one hell of a sweat, and by the time the first of the post vans came steam-rolling down Rathbone Place at 5 a.m. and Lew Levy came out and started unfastening the shutters of the caff, I reckoned I'd been staring at the ceiling for the past couple of hours.

What do you do in these circumstances? Well, I read some of *Psmith in the City*, which always seemed to me a work of stark realism rather than the light comedy it's always made out to be, brewed a cup of tea and drank it, listened to some of the odd noises the house made at this time of day, which I always reckoned couldn't come from human beings, and then figured that it mightn't be a bad idea to write up that notice of *Silver Wedding* for the *Crucible*. And do you know, it was just the thing to settle my nerves? Seeing that I hadn't ever written a theatre review before I stuck in a classy phrase or two—'bourgeois angst' was one, and 'undeviating aesthetic line' was another—and by nine o'clock I had 1,200 words or so on the

193

typewriter. Just the kind of stuff Mortimer-Smith would like I said to myself as I read them back, and to celebrate I decided I'd go and have a pair of kippers round the corner at Lew Levy's. I'd hadn't got any money, what with the expenses still owing from the Ramsgate trip and payday not being until Friday, but I reckoned that in the circumstances Lew would stand me a bob's credit, and so it proved.

It was still early and there was no one much in the caff except a postman or two and a plump old girl you sometimes saw in the Wheatsheaf who was supposed to have been Augustus John's mistress around the time of King Edward's coronation, so I chewed away at my kippers, which were fresh for once, and thought about how I could spend the time before I was due at the Black House. Bateman Street, where I hadn't called for a bit, was due a visit, but I opted to take the notice of *Silver Wedding* over to Mortimer-Smith's office in Fitzroy Square. Who knew? If I played my cards right I might get a free drink into the bargain, or at the very least a commission to review some new novel with a title like *Love Among the Daisies*.

As it turned out, I couldn't have been more wrong. When I got to the *Crucible*'s office at around eleven—there was never any point getting there earlier than that—I found Mortimer-Smith standing on the pavement helping a taxi driver load what appeared to be about half a ton of books into the back of a waiting cab. By the look of him he'd clearly had one or two already, and the taxi driver didn't seem as if he were 100 per cent sober either. In fact, he kept dropping the books onto the floor and at one point a copy of J. M. Robertson's

A History of Freethought in the Nineteenth Century went bowling away into the gutter.

'Hello, Jim,' he said, when he saw me. 'What brings you here?'

'Brought that notice of *Silver Wedding*,' I said, taking it out of my jacket pocket.

'Can't help you there, I'm afraid,' Mortimer-Smith said. He picked up a copy of a book called *Such a Tale it is I Have to Tell* and chucked it into the cab.

'What do you mean?'

'Like I said, can't help you, old boy. You'd better give it to the next editor of the *Crucible* when he decides to drop round.'

At this point the penny dropped. 'Order of the bowler hat?' I asked, with as much sympathy as I could muster.

'No, resigned last night,' Mortimer-Smith said. He looked a bit cross. 'I have my pride. You saw this month's, I expect? Between you and me the thing about Madame Blavatsky I could just about stand. It was the essay on bi-metallism I drew the line at. I don't know what's got into Chalkie. I took him out to dinner and tried to drum some sense into him, but it was no good. When he started talking about making the mag a driving force for democratic enlightenment I knew it was all up with a capital U.'

'I see.' Something struck me and I stared a bit at the stack of books. 'What's all this?'

'Retiring editor's perk,' Mortimer-Smith said. 'I'm taking all the review copies off to Gaston's to flog 'em. Want to help? You could have 10 per cent.'

'No thanks,' I said. 'What happened to that

poem, though?'

' "The White Shoulders of My Recumbent Love"? I'm afraid Chalkie thought it was dangerously immoral. I don't think he approves of even married people having sexual relationships.'

At this point the taxi driver gave a kind of groan and dropped a bundle of psychology textbooks all over the pavement, so I decided to leave them to it and wandered off across Fitzroy Square, where the last remnants of the early-morning fog were still hanging over the plane trees. So that was another editorial chum departing. It just went to show. In ordinary circumstances I'd have been pretty soured by this unexpected bombshell, but do you know, I was so excited by the prospect of the evening's excursion and what I might or might not be getting up to with Gladys that I scarcely gave it a thought, just stuck the review of *Silver Wedding* back in my pocket and went off on a long, mooching walk, following the course of the Central Line, along High Holborn to the Rolls Buildings and then ending up in Leather Lane looking at the stuff in the jewellers' windows and thinking that the first thing I'd do when I had a few bob was to buy Gladys a bracelet or one of those diamond clips that really smart girls stuck in their hats. By this time it was about one o'clock and the kipper orgy seemed a long time ago, but thankfully I turned up a couple of threepenny bits in the lining of my jacket and blu'd them on a cup of tea, a doughnut and a single Park Drive out of a machine. That'd keep me going until the evening, I thought, when there'd almost certainly be something to eat at Sir Oswald's pile. Then, would you believe it, I found a penny on the floor next to the Tube which was enough for the bus ride back to Oxford Street. It had started to rain again and there were clouds coming in from the north.

I'd just waltzed through the front door at Rathbone Place and was prodding a packet of Weights someone had dropped on the step to see if there were any fags left in it when, what do you know, the door opposite swung open and a chap stalked out of it as if he was about to enter one of those walking races you see on the newsreels. The post had just arrived—it was lying in a pile on the floor—and by the grace of God the topmost letter was addressed to 'H. Cohen Esq.', so I picked it up and shrilled out: 'I think this one's yours, mate.'

I thought for a second that he was just going to sail on by, but no, he stopped, gave a nod, tore open the envelope, glanced at the letter in it and then stuffed both letter and envelope into the pocket of his coat.

'B——y tarts,' he said bitterly. 'Never leave you alone, eh?'

'That's right,' I said.

'Still raining outside, is it?'

'Not half.'

'Oh well,' he said. 'Be seeing you.' And that was that. Apart from the fact that the twenty or so seconds of our conversation had made it abundantly clear that H. Cohen Esq. wasn't anything to do with the British Union of Fascists, the reason being that he could have made a fair shot at playing Fagin in a stage version of *Oliver Twist*. Still, I reckoned to myself, Haversham was bound to be interested in him, Jew or no Jew, so I bounced up to my room thinking that on the whole it hadn't been a bad kind of a morning. As to what sort of evening lay in wait, God only knew, but as I saw it there was nothing to do but take it as it came. While I was lying on the bed having a smoke from a packet of Weights I'd found under the pillow, and then getting into my evening clothes—there was a dirty great hole in the collar, but I inked it in with a fountain pen—I tried to remember some of the tricks I'd learned as a mess waiter, but it had all been a long time ago and the only thing that came to mind was opening the bottles of red wine half an hour before you intended to serve them, in case some ass said, 'Waiter, this wine's stone cold; take it away and warm it,' and knowing where the gents was, and—if things got really desperate— pretending you had a cleft palate and couldn't talk properly. As for the degrees of social exaltation that might be on offer at Savehay Farm, I wasn't too fussed. As the Old Lady used to say, us Rosses have always known how to move in the best circles; it's just that we don't very often get the opportunity.

Anyway, what with brooding about H. Cohen Esq. and the month I'd spent as junior waiter in the officers' mess at Eastbourne—they were a low lot, you know, all counter-jumping ex-NCOs who dropped their aitches and spat out bits of gristle on the side of their plates—the time passed pretty quickly, and come half past four I put a coat on top of my evening suit and set out for the King's Road. It had stopped raining, the afternoon had begun to fade away and it was one of those queer times just before the offices start closing when the West End streets are full of women coming home from shopping and schoolgirls in blazers with hockey sticks trailing after them and mysterious old blokes bending down to pick up fag ends and then looking

198

guiltily up when they catch your eye.

As I wandered down into Oxford Street past a restaurant called Vincenzi's, a chap I knew slightly called Fitzalan-Jones—he did highbrow broadcasts for the BBC and wrote a column for *John O'London's* called 'Metroland Musings'— dashed out, hailed a taxi and was borne away in the same ten seconds or so, and I thought to myself, lucky b——, probably off to some furnished flat in Kensington where Miss Eulalie Belchamber is waiting for him with the lights turned down and nothing on but a welcoming expression. Wouldn't have surprised me if the BBC was paying for the cab fare either. Curiously the sight of Fitzalan-Jones cruising off west depressed me no end, because it reminded me that I hadn't two halfpence to rub together until payday and the chances of anyone asking me to give a talk on the BBC were slightly worse than Brenda Dean Paul being given a prize for sobriety and general good conduct. Still, there's nothing like a brisk walk for putting things in perspective, and by the time I reached the top end of Shaftesbury Avenue I'd cheered up a bit. It was getting mistier and the light was beginning to go, the kind of time when you light a fag just to reassure yourself you're alive, and I was just in sight of the Underground steps at Piccadilly when all of a sudden a blonde woman, slim-backed and on the tallish side, came into view framed by the glow of a shop window and I stopped dead in my tracks.

'Gladys!'

She blinked a bit before she registered it was me—here's another one like Marjorie, I thought, who wouldn't wear glasses unless you paid her—but then she smiled and marched across, with her high heels clattering on the pavement like a blacksmith doing overtime at work in the forge. Oddly enough, she looked a bit less well turned out than the last time I'd seen her, and there was a spot starting up on her chin next to the birthmark. Needless to say, this had precisely the same effect on me as the Pools winner who discovers that he's won £12,998 rather than thirteen thousand.

'It's beastly cold, isn't it?' she said.

'Beastly cold,' I agreed. It was actually quite a mild night. There were half a dozen things I wanted to say to her, but I had an idea that most of them ought to wait until we were back on the sofa, or at least on licensed premises. She'd caught sight of the evening suit under my coat by now.

'You're all dressed up tonight,' she said, all mock-maidenly.

'It's the school Old Boys' dinner,' I improvised gamely. 'Don't usually go, but this year some chums of mine persuaded me.' The last thing I wanted was her finding out about the trip to Savehay Farm. 'Did you have a good time away?'

'It wasn't too bad,' she said vaguely.

'I got your letter,' I said.

'Oh *that*,' she said, and I couldn't for the life of me work out whether this was maidenly modesty blushingly at work, or whether she meant the letter had been a terrible mistake and would I disregard everything it said.

We were still standing in the middle of the pavement, which meant that anyone coming by had to swerve to one side, so I took the opportunity of steering her into a shop doorway—a souvenir shop, it was, displaying several pictures of Queen Mary looking like a rather bewildered sheep. Once

I'd got her there I made sure I held on to her arm. Then I realized I was in a bit of a jam. She clearly didn't want to talk about the letter, which would have been my main line of attack. Plus I was due at the Black House in half an hour. All of a sudden, though, a fine line of attack occurred to me.

'I saw your friend Florence the other day,' I said.

'Florence who?'

'Florence Risborough, isn't she called?'

The look she shot back was exactly like Greta Garbo's when the police say they've called for her husband and they don't mind waiting if he's out. 'I don't think I know anyone called Florence Risborough.'

'Yes, you do,' I insisted. 'The girl you were talking to outside the Café Polska that afternoon.'

'Oh, is that her name? Florence Risborough? Where did you meet her?'

'Oh, in a pub or somewhere,' I said. I reckoned I'd better keep shtum about the co-respondent's trip to Ramsgate. 'Look'—there was a clock on the other side of Shaftesbury Avenue saying 4.45 and I knew I only had three-quarters of an hour to get to the Black House—'I could come round and see you tonight if you liked.'

'Yes,' she said, a bit thoughtfully, 'I'd like that.'

'It'd be a bit on the late side. Those Old Boys' dinners have a habit of going on,' I added, just to be on the safe side.

'I don't get back until after eleven anyway,' she said, and I'm not saying there was that bold look in her eye that the Old Lady used to warn me about in my dealings with women, but I can tell you the Tennyson poem that immediately sprang to mind was the one about the lotus-eaters. Or maybe the

Meredith one about being hot for certainties. There was a chap who knew all about the way a chap's liable to get treated by the opposite sex.

'I'll come round then,' I said. 'Providing you don't send out for Hercules again.'

'Oh no,' she said seriously. 'There won't be any Hercules.' There was definitely the makings of a spot on the end of her chin. 'Why don't you do that?'

Naturally, I didn't remember a great deal about the walk to the Black House. A couple of airships could have come down in Green Park for all I'd have noticed. There was no one much about when I got there—even the porter had disappeared from the front steps, which were sunk in gloom—but just inside the doorway I bumped into Blennerhassett, practically glowing with suppressed excitement and, like me, wearing evening dress.

'Hang on,' I asked. 'Are you on this game as well?'

'That's right,' Blennerhassett said. He'd put dressing on his hair and slicked it back, which made him look like a self-important hamster. 'Mr Baxter said they were short-handed, so I volunteered. It sounds terribly exciting.'

It sounded a pain in the neck to me, but I reckoned the sobersides, are-we-fit-for-our-task approach was what was needed, so I pulled myself up—I was eight inches taller than Blennerhassett in any case—and demanded: 'Got any experience of this kind of work?'

'Not really,' Blennerhassett said. 'But Mr Baxter said he was sure I could pick it up in no time.'

We'll see about that, I thought to myself, but before I could say anything else Baxter himself came bristling up, wearing an evening suit with a white waistcoat that made him look a bit like the maître d' on gala night at the Florida. He was clearly as nervous as hell about something, and when he caught sight of us he practically purred with enthusiasm. 'Ah, Blennerhassett, Ross. Delighted to see you.' He looked at his watch. 'We should be leaving in about ten minutes. Any gen you need before we go?'

Blennerhassett wondered who the mysterious guest might be, but Baxter soon shushed him up. 'Entirely confidential,' he said. 'More than my job's worth to tell even you chaps. Security, you understand.'

We understood. At least, I did. Blennerhassett, on the other hand, looked like a fox terrier who's just been told that, no, he won't be going for a walk. There were one or two other people hanging about in the hall who I didn't recognize, but no sign of Davenport, who I'd rather been hoping would be on the trip. As we were filing out into the backyard, where there was a van parked up by the gates and a surprisingly large number of crates of empty milk bottles, Baxter gave me a friendly nod and said: 'Shame to take you with us tonight, Ross.'

'Why's that, sir?'

'Operation Clean-Up should be in full swing. Routing out the fleshpots of Soho and making the whoremasters pay. Lot of our chaps headed that way, I believe.'

'I shall be sorry to miss it, sir,' I said.

I was as well. In fact, hearing about Operation Clean-Up and the chaps who were headed down to Soho made me think I ought to get on the blower to Haversham before you could say Rudolf Valentino was a sheeny. After all, if Haversham had advance warning about Davenport and his friends cruising through Soho he could do something about it, and guess who'd get the credit? The question was: how to let him know? By this time we were sitting in the van—me, Blennerhassett, Baxter and two of the chaps I'd seen hanging about in the hall—with the driver, togged up in Blackshirt gear, already revving the engine, so there was no chance of doubling back inside in search of a telephone. No doubt there'd be one at Savehay Farm, but all I could do for the moment was sit tight. And so, as the van ground on towards Ealing, as Blennerhassett and Baxter chewed the fat about the National Government, and the two other chaps—they were professional waiters, I discovered, hired for the evening—talked about Murray and Mooney's last show at the Shepherd's Bush Empire, I sat staring at the West London shopfronts, all aflame with artificial light, the crowds of people hanging around at street corners and behind them the rows of mean little houses disappearing into the murk.

It had been about quarter to six when we left, but what with the traffic and a wrong turning somewhere near Acton High Street it was nearly seven by the time we got into the countryside proper. What sort of place was Savehay Farm, I asked Baxter, and he said, oh, it was the country pile where Sir Oswald spent his weekends, all done up in the latest style, didn't you know, after which he looked a bit grim, whereupon I remembered reading in the paper that Lady Cynthia had died earlier that year of appendicitis, or something, and something else, which hadn't appeared in the papers, to the effect that the grieving husband had been carrying on something shocking with a bright young aristocratic sprig young enough to be his daughter. You have to hand it to chaps like that, you know. Half their success is down to simple cheek.

Anyhow, it was 7.30 by the time we roared into the courtyard at Savehay Farm, and Baxter was practically writhing with nerves. There wasn't much time for sightseeing, so keen was he for us to be straightaway rushed inside, but I caught sight of a couple of Daimlers parked at the end of the drive under the care of a tall chap in a bowler, while a couple of other blokes stood smoking fags a little way off and exchanging backchat with a housemaid who'd brought out tea on a tray. All this increased a suspicion I'd been incubating from the moment I'd first seen Baxter at the Black House an hour and a half back, which was that something a bit out of the ordinary was going on. And sure enough, the servants' quarters where we fetched up was like an anthill, with people tearing about bawling for footmen, trays of ice being rushed back and forth and an old butler vainly trying to keep order. Just the kind of atmosphere in which you could sneak out and use the phone without anyone noticing, I thought to myself, but Baxter instantly marched us off into a kind of pantry where someone had left a Scrabble board on the table (interestingly, the first two words I noticed were SEXUAL and INTERCOURSE) and told us to wait there until he came back.

'I say,' Blennerhassett squeaked, 'did you see those cars? One of them was flying some kind of standard, or I'm not much mistaken.'

'I expect it's King Zog, over on a state visit,' I

said, just to take him down a peg or two. Beyond the pantry there was a glimpse of a long carpeted passage. It was now or never, I thought.

'Back in a moment,' I said.

'Where are you going?' Blennerhassett asked. He looked faintly scandalized by this dereliction of duty.

'Gents,' I explained.

One of the hired waiters was telling the other that the band at the Savoy might not be any b——y good, but the tips weren't bad. Out in the passage I headed due east and came to a hallway where a vague-looking woman with a pair of pince-nez balanced on the bridge of her nose was absent-mindedly inspecting some flowers in a pot.

'Sorry to trouble you madam,' I improvised, 'but is there a telephone I might use? I'm afraid there's a case of champagne that the wine merchants don't seem to have sent up.'

Thankfully the old girl didn't seem to be too put out by this request, and a moment or two later I was in a smallish apartment, halfway between a library and a gun room, staring at a photograph of a grim old boy standing next to a kind of funeral mound of dead partridges, and asking the operator to put me through to West End Central.

After what seemed like an eternity, a voice suddenly blared out: 'Duty Sergeant.'

'Is Mr Haversham there, please?'

'Who wants 'im?'

'This is Mr Ross.'

There was another echoing silence and then the voice said: 'Is that Ross spelled R-o-s-s or with an 'e'?'

'R-o-s-s, of course,' I told him. 'Would you get

206

Mr Haversham, please? It's very important.'

'All right, all right. Keep your hair on. Only we had the Earl of Rosse in here the other day. Very nice young gentleman, 'e was, once he'd sobered up.'

'Christ!' I said. There were footsteps coming through the house. In another half-minute or so I'd have company. 'Please can you get Mr Haversham? There's something important which he needs to know about.'

'E's not here,' the voice said. 'You want me to tell him anything?'

The footsteps were getting close. 'Tell him Operation Clean-Up is booked for this evening.' Then I remembered that there was a pretty good chance Haversham wouldn't know what Operation Clean-Up was. 'Tell him there's going to be trouble in Soho with the Blackshirts.'

'Oh *that*,' the voice said, as if I'd just told him Arsenal played in red and white. 'Got half a dozen blokes down in Wardour Street right this minute . . .'

'And if those Bath Oliver biscuits aren't here by half past eight we shall have to consider closing our account,' I yelled, and then put the phone down as the old girl with the pince-nez came floating back into the room. Ten seconds later I was haring back down the passage to the pantry, where Baxter, who'd clearly just arrived there, fixed me with an absolutely gimlet eye and demanded to know where the hell I'd been.

'Taken short, sir,' I explained. 'Had to find the gents.'

'Well, don't let it happen again,' Baxter said. 'If there's one thing we can't have this evening it's

207

slackness.'

Something seemed expected of us, so we chorused: 'No, sir.'

'Right then, follow me.'

And so, led by Baxter, we trudged off down another passage, past a double door which he helpfully explained was the route to the kitchen, and then into a vast, panelled dining room with a dozen wine glasses sparkling in the light of a chandelier, and the old butler laying out decanters of claret. There was a group of men lounging by the fireplace at the far end and I glanced up as they came into view. The tall chap with the moustache and the supercilious expression I recognized instantly as our host for the evening. But standing next to him, with one foot on the fender, was a shortish character with tow-coloured hair who seemed even more familiar. Fact is, I'd seen his face a thousand times, in the illustrated papers, on the sides of china mugs, laying a wreath once at the Cenotaph flanked by a couple of dozen red-coated guardsmen. And several hundred million people around the Empire, from the chap in the scarlet tunic cantering down the Yukon trail to the *babu* loitering on the Calcutta pavement, could have said the same. It was Edward Albert Christian George Andrew Patrick David Saxe-Coburg, better known to you, me and his loyal subjects around the world as the Prince of Wales.

13

ALL IN THE LINE OF DUTY

The wind blows over Soho Square
And into Carlisle Street
The rain will follow on its heels
Mixing into sleet.

James Ross, Soho Eclogues

Have you ever waited at table? I wonder. The trick, a month's experience in B Coy mess Southern Command insists, is to be unobtrusive and attentive. If a chap looks up from his plate with a peevish expression on his face, then you nip forward, decanter at the ready. If not, you keep your mouth shut and stay out of the way. And if the chap who looks up with the peevish expression happens to be the Prince of Wales you nip forward twice as fast. Anyhow, ten minutes into the spread at Savehay Farm, I didn't reckon I was doing too badly. The soup had been in and gone out again, and we were about to start ferrying over the fish. The gentlemen were drinking Sauternes (very good Sauternes it was too—I'd had a swig behind the door when I thought no one was looking) and the only crisis that had occurred so far was when an old chap with a pepper-and-salt moustache asked if there was any Tabasco.

Sir Oswald had already lowered his second glass of wine (with yours truly noting the glint in his eye and bounding forward like Eddie Hapgood on the wing) and the Prince had got through at least three bread rolls. The only minor problem was Blennerhassett, who hadn't the least idea what he was doing. Already he'd pressed a glass of wine on another old chap who'd asked for tonic water, and whacked two plates together with an almighty clang that sounded like the last trump. You could see that he intended to dine out on this for the next ten years, and when the Prince leaned forward at one point and asked if there was any more butter he practically fainted over the cruet.

Meanwhile, in the intervals of sprinting out to the passage and through the double doors to see if there were any more plates arriving on the hot tray, and nodding to the cook—a tough-looking old pantomime dame who must have been a yard around the hips—I was keeping my ears open. Haversham, I knew, would give his eye teeth for a transcript of what Mosley was saying, so I stationed myself half a dozen feet from the back of his chair. The strange thing, though, was that Mosley and the Prince didn't seem to be hitting it off. Or rather, they couldn't find a topic both of them felt like discussing. Sir Oswald tried his guest with Count Meinsdorff, only for HRH to favour him with what Lady Furness thought of a nightclub called the Blue Lagoon. Sir Oswald came back with some sage remarks about the encouraging situation in Italy, only for HRH to ask what he thought of the new line in gentleman's hats that Lock was selling. Sir Oswald quoted some nifty statistics about how his boys were doing in organizing the unemployed miners of Merthyr Tydfil, only for HRH to note that half a dozen ladies of his acquaintance had assured him that hemlines were likely to go on rising. This went on for some time, with the other chaps sitting nearby saying things like 'Indeed?' and 'Hear, hear', but there wasn't anything there for Haversham to take an interest in. The only thing I could have said for certain was how little I fancied the sight of Sir Oswald, who behaved exactly like the villain in *Dulcie's Ruin*, had a pair of popping black eyes you'd have run a mile from and, from the expression on his face when he picked up his knife and fork, looked as if he'd had enough of soup, fish and cutlets and only human flesh would do.

And oddly enough, despite the sight of Mosley's moustache hanging over the soup six feet away, and the Prince's high, washed-out voice answering him—he spoke that queer brand of gentleman's cockney where 'nothing' comes out as *nudding* and 'whatever' as *woddever*—it was all I could do to pay attention, what with all the other things I was quietly stewing about. For a start, there was whatever might be going on in Dean Street. Then, curiously enough, there was Gladys and the dance she was leading me, and what I was going to do about it? There was even, at the back of my mind, the memory of the *Crucible* going west and what was I going to do about that. All in all I was in one hell of a state, and if Mosley had announced that he intended to rally thousands of unemployed miners, march on Parliament and declare a state of martial law, I doubt I'd have even heard him.

And then something happened which drove all thought of Dean Street, Gladys and the pointlessness of writing any more poems until there was someone to publish them clean out of my head. We'd taken out the remains of the fish— and I can report that HRH had a shockingly bad

211

appetite—and were just bringing in the cutlets, which the cook had swamped in some horribly pungent sauce, when Blennerhassett, in his eagerness to serve the royal guest, tripped over his own feet and deposited plate, cutlets and sauce all over the Prince's waistcoat.

What generally happens in these circumstances is an embarrassed silence, followed by a corking row. This time round was no exception. The Prince gave a little start and then struggled hastily to his feet as a cutlet went slithering down onto the carpet by his chair. Mosley seemed a bit amused and then, as if suddenly aware of the enormity of the outrage committed in his own dining room, went absolutely scarlet. Baxter looked aghast, as if a headless spectre had just laid a bony paw on his shoulder. Blennerhassett, on the other hand, seemed as if he might be about to burst into tears. You could see him staring at the Prince, the upended plate and the ruined waistcoat with a kind of dreadful anguish, as if he'd just committed a treasonable offence rather than temporarily inconveniencing some butter-haired old snob who, if you asked me, needed all the inconveniencing he could get.

Anyhow, after about five seconds of this an absolute fusillade of chatter broke out, with Blennerhassett shrilling how terribly sorry he was, and Mosley calling for the butler and half a dozen people offering napkins and handkerchiefs. Oddly, the Prince didn't seem too put out. He simply stood there, while the sauce from the cutlets continued to ooze off his waistcoat, with his hands slightly raised and a sort of bemused expression on his face. Ten seconds later I was shepherding him out into the passage. Ten seconds after that I had him parked on a chair that someone had placed next to the double doors that led to the kitchen and was sponging him down with a couple of towels that Baxter, looking as if he'd just signed his own death warrant, had managed to procure from somewhere. The thing that struck me most, by the way, was what a tiny chap he was: he couldn't have been more than nine stone and looked as if he hadn't had a square meal in weeks. There was silence for a bit, apart from the noise of yours truly scrubbing away at his shirt front, and then he said: 'Dashed awkward thing to have happened.'

'That's right, sir.'

'Chap that did it seemed frightfully nervous, I should say.'

'Bound to be in the circumstances, sir.'

'Actually,' he said, 'I think there might be a spare waistcoat in the car. My man generally packs another set of clothes, you know.'

I liked that 'you know' for its air of all-of-us-in-this-together good fellowship, as if he and I and Lady Cunard would shortly be off to the Embassy club for a go at the lobster thermidor while Noël Coward warbled his latest in our ears as we ate.

'I'll have someone go and look, sir,' I told him.

Happily the butler was at hand with a pop-eyed footman or two, and in a couple of minutes they'd kitted him out with some fresh togs. When he emerged from the room where they'd taken him off to change I was still hanging about, and he said: 'I say, thanks awfully.'

'Not at all, sir.'

'All in the line of duty, I suppose?'

'That's right, sir.'

'Ex-serviceman I take it?'

'Up to a point, sir.'

And then, would you believe it, he put his hand in his trouser pocket, fished around for a moment or two, and then presented me with half a crown.

As for the rest of the evening at Savehay Farm, it was as big a frost as an Arctic ice floe. There was a bit of a chat about German re-armament, in the course of which HRH opined that he'd always found the Huns 'most polite', and a nerve-grinding ten minutes or so when Mosley sounded off about all the tip-top schemes that were currently on his mind (India, the unemployed, the National Debt, and an odd-sounding scheme for collecting up unused stamps) while the Prince sat there simply squirming with boredom, but by half past ten the last of the plates had been cleared away and the ashtrays emptied and the whole thing was over. The last thing I remember is the sight of Mosley, positively bristling up at an old chap who asked him a question about Musso, as if only his duty as a host forbade him from taking the old boy out into the yard and cutting his head off. Outside in the yard the moon had got up, drenching the courtyard with blue-black light, and the two private detectives were leaning on the bonnet of the Daimler smoking cigars.

'Lot of hanging around in this job,' I said, as we traipsed past.

'You should come along on the nights he goes to see Lady Furness,' one of them said. 'Never get home until three.'

Back in the van I got the impression that things hadn't been what you might call a success. Baxter was rightfully aggrieved, the two hired waiters were in a sulk about some bonus that had been promised them and then withdrawn, while Blennerhassett still looked as if he might be about to burst into tears.

'I'm most terribly sorry, sir,' he said to Baxter as soon as we were in our seats and the driver was turning the van—he damn near crashed into the Daimler, too.

'Can't be helped, Blennerhassett,' Baxter said.

'Do you think, sir, that I ought to write to His Royal Highness and apologize?'

'I think he'd find it a great consolation, Blennerhassett.'

This, by the way, was the only time I ever heard Baxter make a joke.

Anyway, after this Blennerhassett cheered up no end. There'd been people like him in B Coy, meek little clerks from Clapham and Croydon, with the scent of blood in their nostrils, just itching to man a barricade and get a lump of shrapnel in their guts into the bargain. As for me, I positively gloomed away thinking about the Toreador, which was probably in flames by now, and Gladys taking her ease in the second-floor back at Meard Street, and Haversham's black-olive eyes staring expressionlessly at me in the room at West End Central.

There wasn't much traffic about, and we were back in the King's Road by a quarter to twelve. The waiters vanished like a couple of rats up a drain, Blennerhassett hurried off to see if he could get the last Tube, Baxter disappeared into the Black House and I was left with the driver.

'Where's this bus going now?' I asked.

'Back to the depot in Mile End.'

'Any chance of a lift?'

'Where to?'

215

'Anywhere near Oxford Street.'

'Be my guest.'

'You're a gent.'

He was a canny old bloke of about sixty-five with an Old Bill moustache. Chatty, too, and by the time we got to Oxford Circus I'd heard all about his sciatica and what his wife thought of Ethel M. Dell. Anyhow, he was as good as his word and dropped me just next to Bourne & Hollingsworth, and there I was—it was about a minute or two before midnight—making my way through Soho Square, where the drunks were kicking up no end of a racket and an old chap with a parchment face and a dog collar who'd plainly had a tremendous amount to drink was standing on a street corner belting out, 'Anyone here seen sneaking Judas?' to the tune of 'What shall we do with the drunken sailor?' at the top of his voice.

Dean Street, when I got to it, was as quiet as the grave. To be sure, someone had chucked the contents of a coster's barrow over the pavement at the far end, and one of the windows in the Cadenza had a hole in it, but apart from that you could have held a vicarage tea party there and not been incommoded. Walking past the Toreador, where you could hear the band playing 'Sweet Little Coochie Coo', I saw Edgar standing half in and half out of the doorway.

'Quiet night?'

'Seen worse,' Edgar said. 'Couple of hooligans started mixing it in the card room, but that Maurice—you know, the lad as used to box at the Queen's 'all—laid one of them out as neat as ninepence, and after that they went off quiet as lambs. Ho yuss. No, it was the Cadenza as had all the trouble.'

'What sort of trouble?'

A vaguely distinguished-looking chap in a tall hat came sauntering down the steps and Edgar tapped his forehead with the point of his finger. 'Night, Sir Archibald.'

'Well, about nine o'clock there's this great lot of shouting started up. Elvie in the cloakroom says, "You leave it be, Edgar, it's nothing to do with us," and I would have done too, but in the end Mr Samuelson sends up from his office to ask what's going on, so I reckoned I'd take a look. Anyway, there's half a dozen blokes on the pavement kicking up no end of a din, and then, would you believe it, the winders start opening up at top and the ta—the young ladies—are giving them an earful back. After that the perlice turn up and there's a barney on the doorstep. You never saw anything like it.'

'Any idea what it was all about?'

'I yerd tell,' Edgar said, 'that it was some of them Blackshirts. But if you want my opinion, it was Bolshevists causing trouble.'

'Anyone arrested?'

'Was a perlice van turned up,' Edgar said hoarsely, 'but then a chap got stuck in the washroom here—you know what them catches is like—and I had to go and help him out.'

For some reason—God knows why—I felt an overwhelming sense of relief that the Toreador hadn't been smashed up.

'You coming in for a drink?' Edgar said. He looked more than ever like one of the gargoyles you see on the parapet of Westminster Cathedral. 'That young lady as was here when you had all that trouble's at the bar, I b'lieve.'

In ordinary circumstances I'd have leaped at the chance to catch up with Marjorie, who I hadn't seen since the night I ended up in the cell at West End Central, but somehow I didn't feel like it. Besides, a mad idea had just occurred to me. 'No thanks,' I said. 'Early night for me, I reckon.'

'Early nights,' Edgar said, as I turned off down Dean Street—he clearly thought it was one hell of a joke. 'Early nights! I've 'ad 'em.'

I bet you have, I thought to myself, not looking back. The mad idea, you won't be surprised to learn, was to head for Meard Street. The way I figured it was that Gladys would either be there, as she'd suggested, and want to see me, or not be in, in which case she'd never know I'd called. There was, of course, a third possibility, which was that she'd be there and not want to see me, but I can't say the thought crossed my mind. After all, a girl who writes you a letter telling you she's dying to see you isn't exactly going to slam the door in your face, is she?

Anyhow, I'd just said goodbye to Edgar, who was staring pensively out into the night the way Jack Buchanan does when he's about to burst into song when I noticed that the far end of Dean Street was suddenly turning populous again. To be exact, there were three burly-looking chaps with what looked like hockey sticks in their fists thundering past the front door of the Nellie Dean. As they hurried up I made a second discovery, which that the front pair were Caraway and Stevens, the two likely lads who I'd done the unarmed combat session with at the Black House. What do you do in such circumstances? The obvious thing was to beat a hasty retreat down Dean Street, but that would have meant leaving Edgar, who'd already retired to a vantage point halfway inside the door, to repel boarders. By this time, too, the hockey-stick brigade was a bare ten yards away, yelling as they came. The only thing to do, I reckoned, was to play decoy, so nipping back into the arc of light that fell out of the Toreador's front door—Edgar had vanished now, and I couldn't say I blamed him—I stuck my hand up in front of my face like a policeman directing traffic and bawled out in the toniest accent I could muster: 'I say, you chaps! Better late than never, what?'

Anyway, they came grinding to a halt, looking a bit puzzled and none too pleased, until by the grace of God Caraway gave me a nod of recognition.

'Couldn't be helped,' he said with horrible earnestness. 'You know Stevens here? This is Mackintosh.' Mackintosh grinned prawnishly—he was built on exactly the same scale as the others. 'Got held up in Lexington Street. Frightful to-do, and only just got clear. What's happening here?'

'Nothing,' I said, with a fair stab at matey confidentiality. 'Baxter told me to hang on until the reinforcements turned up. Know your way around here, do you?'

Nobody did, so I filled them in on the Toreador's topography, hoping all the while that Edgar had had the sense to bolt the double doors and call the police. I was just proposing that it might be a sound idea to go and turn over the tables in the card room when Mackintosh, who could happily have understudied King Kong, whacked his calf with the hockey stick and yelled out, no by God, why didn't we go and smash up the ballroom, that'd show the

219

yid who ran the place once and for all?

Next moment we were through the doors, which Edgar hadn't managed to lock, and sprinting through the Toreador's vestibule with waiters diving for cover and Elvie, who was just passing through on her way to the cloakroom, shrieking for dear life and dropping dozens of packets of fags on the floor. The only thing that might play to our advantage, I reckoned, was the fact that they were all clearly as drunk as lords. On the other hand even a drunk can handle a hockey stick and Mackintosh by this stage was having a terrific time knocking lumps out of a rather tasteful statue of Terpsichore, or it may have been Bacchus, which Sammy had had put up in the alcove by the ballroom doors, while Caraway hammered away at a reproduction of some pre-Raphaelite painting of Ariadne attended by her handmaidens at the bath.

Do you know that sensation you get when you seem to be looking down on everything from a great height, and even though you might be in the middle of the most fearful chaos everything around you has a curiously abstract quality? Well, that was how it felt just now. The Toreador was in pandemonium, with women in off-the-shoulder dresses running in all directions screaming like stuck pigs as they went and their gentlemen attendants, who were mostly on the elderly side, making feeble attempts to intervene. Sammy appeared halfway down the staircase, just as Caraway, who'd clearly had enough of belabouring Ariadne's outsize torso, brought down half a chandelier, and I gave him a kind of 'I'm-doing-my-best-in-very-difficult-circumstances' gesture, which I doubt for a moment he took in. What with the screams, and the smash of the chandelier and the noise of the band, who were still thundering away in the ballroom, there was precious little opportunity for rational thought, but all of a sudden my eye fell on the door that led down to the basement and an idea occurred to me.

'Down here,' I yelled, managing to catch Caraway's and Mackintosh's eyes at the same time—where Stevens was I didn't know. 'Office in the basement. Get the safe while we're at it, eh?'

For some reason—no doubt the amount they'd had to drink—they jumped at the idea. Caraway swung the door open and the three of us simply plunged down the rickety staircase like Rollicking Bill the Sailor and his friends gone to man the bilge pumps. 'This way,' I yelled again, in the tone of a master-strategist who knows exactly what he's doing, and a moment later we were tearing into the basement where, as I knew, the furnishings consisted of a table, a typewriter, a sealed strongbox that was welded to the floor, a filing cabinet, and an open door whose key I took the opportunity of locking as I doubled round and made my way smartly back up the stairs

*   *   *

Twenty minutes later, with a glass of champagne that Sammy had presented me with kicking up stink in my insides, I found myself out on the pavement in Dean Street. There was a police van parked outside the Toreador and a hell of a lot of noise still coming from within, but I'd done my bit and I reckoned what I did with myself now was my own affair. They'd caught Stevens, too, and by the time I left Maurice had been sitting on his

221

chest just outside the ladies' lavatory. It was long past midnight now, and to tell you the truth I was pretty near dead on my feet. But it was worse than that, really. Truth to tell, I was fed up with Soho, and not just because of the BUF trying to smash up Sammy's club. Never mind the late nights and rattling doorknobs in Brewer Street and Lew Levy's chicory essence coffee, I'd got this feeling, which I don't often have, that I was pouring my immortal spirit down the drain a flagon at a time.

Now, that may sound odd, what with some of the dead-end jobs I've done in the past few years. All I can say is that I'd never felt it when I was teaching fretwork in the boys' school that time, or officiating as lifeguard at Brixton Lido, or selling carpet-cleaning lotion door to door in Bayswater. It was funny, but there you are. At the same time, all this anxiety was pretty much quelled by the thought that I was off to see Gladys in the second-floor back. Christ! I thought to myself as I turned the corner into Meard Street. Here's a chap who's just mopped cutlet sauce off the waistcoat of the heir to the throne, not to mention listening to Sir Oswald Mosley droning on about German re-armament and breaking up a nightclub raid single-handed.

Anyway, I turned my pass key in the lock, pressed on the push light—it only lasted about twenty seconds, but I reckoned that would get me as far as the switch outside Mrs Wisbeach's—but there was music coming out from under the door of the first-floor back and, would you believe, just as I came up level with it the door opened and a big foreign-looking bloke with a bald head stepped out onto the landing.

"'Ang on,' this apparition said, in faultless

cockney. 'This ain't the f——g hundred-yard dash. Aren't you the rent bloke?'

'That's me,' I said.

'Glad I seen you then. In fact, I've bin listening out in case you called round.'

The fact that it was about half past midnight and I clearly wasn't out collecting the rents didn't seem to bother him. Perhaps it was just the odd hours he kept that meant I'd never set eyes on him before. There was a split second when I almost told him what he could do with himself, but then, flipping my hand onto the pocket of the coat I'd been wearing over my evening suit, what did I find but Sammy's receipt book.

'Four pounds and four I make it,' Sibierski said and, extraordinarily enough, he dug his hand into his trouser pocket and pulled out four Bradburys and a couple of two-bob bits. Then, while I was writing out the receipt—which was dead difficult, what with the light going off and having to be revived—he looked a bit knowing and said: 'Rum old go this evening?'

'What's that then?' I said, trying to remember if you spelt 'Sibierski' with two 'i's or three.

'You've had dealings with the old girl next door I take it?'

'Mrs Wisbeach?'

'That's her. Always boiling up 'addocks and stinking the place out. Well, round about seven I open the door and there's a pile of cases laid out on the landing, along with her and the oiliest little nigger you ever saw standing there looking as if they'd just robbed a bank. Next thing you know a taxi turns up and away they go. It's my belief they were doing a flit.'

Curiously, the thought that Mrs Wisbeach and Mr Laal might have left Meard Street together didn't bother me in the least. Good luck to the old girl was how I saw it, though it'd be a shame to say goodbye to the Pekoe Points. Anyway, I had another mission in mind. Sibierski had disappeared behind his front door now, so I carried on up the stairs. The push light had gone out again but oddly the door of Gladys's flat was an inch or two open and a line of orange light was spilling out over the landing. As I'd suspected she was at home, and not gone to bed either by the look of it. For once the fates weren't going to move the finishing line another ten yards down the track just as I ran up to breast it.

Anyhow, I rapped a couple of times on the door, which opened an inch or two more. There was no sound from inside, so I gave another knock. This time I was sure I heard a voice say something— whether it was 'come in' or 'f—— off' I couldn't make out—so I pulled the door open to its fullest extent and marched into the flat. It took me a second or two to establish my bearings, and for a moment, looking round the room, I had an idea that I was wrong about the voice and the place was empty. But no, there was definitely something moving about on the sofa. Two things, in fact. They were Gladys and Davenport, the knuckleduster merchant from the King's Road, and there wasn't the slightest doubt what they were doing.

14

OUTWARD BOUND

Let's have a glass of best bitter, boys
Let's have a tumbler of gin
Let's have squint in the doorway
Of the Marlborough Street Palace of Sin.

James Ross, Soho Eclogues

It was one of those dull, godforsaken mornings in early November, with a breeze blowing in from the west that would have scraped limpets off a rock and I was sitting in a caff at the bottom end of Argyll Place, feeling like hell and watching a dustcart go by. The wind kept on blowing and the faces of the people passing on the other side of the window had that grim, whey-faced look they got around this time of the year, and I thought to myself that steering a corporation dustcart—it was one of those big ones with space in the back for Wembley Stadium's rubbish after the Cup Final—wasn't such a bad job. Just at this moment a bloke in a flat cap with a face streaked with dirt like a nigger minstrel upended a bin into the back and a can of tuna fish fell out onto the pavement, all of which reminded me of Gladys again, I suppose, and must have turned my face even gloomier than it had been a couple of minutes before. On the next table there was a copy of the *Daily Sketch*, open at a headline that said: ARTHUR AND EUNICE AITCHISON—OUR TIPS FOR A HAPPY MARRIAGE.

225

'Come on, son,' Haversham said. He was stirring what might have been his fifth lump of sugar into a cup of tea. 'Brace up. You look like the chap who's just swallowed the joey out of the Christmas pudding.'

'Sorry,' I said. 'Not feeling too good.' It was the truth as well. Four o'clock that morning I'd still been lying awake in Rathbone Place thinking about what I'd seen in Meard Street the night before.

'Christ,' Haversham said. He was wearing the same brown suit and his black eyes were darting around in his head like minnows trying to evade a pike. 'What do they put in this b——g tea, I'd like to know?'

We'd been in the caff a quarter of an hour now, Haversham telling me about the fun they'd had in Dean Street the night before, me telling him about my exploits at Savehay Farm. Queerly enough, he was a lot less impressed with my account of sponging cutlet sauce off the heir to the throne than I'd expected him to be.

'All very well hobnobbing with the Prince of Wales,' he said. 'Make a nice story, I don't doubt. But it's not as if he came out with anything any one didn't already know.'

'B——y hell,' I said. 'I volunteered for all that at great personal inconvenience, rang you up to tell you about the Soho clean-up when . . . when my life could have been in danger, and I've now supplied a full report of everything that was said. Is that all the thanks I get?'

'Hold on, hold on,' Haversham said, his eyes keeling around like drunken sailors. I didn't know whether he was highly amused or seriously cross. 'No need to get like that. It's good work. Can't fault

226

you for initiative. But we've the devil of a problem doing anything with Mosley, now the newspapers're so sweet on him and HRH is drinking his brandy cocktails. All sorts of covert influences being brought to bear. What we want is some dirt on the people running his errands, if you take my meaning.'

'What about that Davenport bloke?' I said. After all, there was someone I'd happily see in Holloway as soon as could be arranged. 'You can run him in, surely?'

'Can't be done,' Haversham said. 'Nothing to go on, is there? Busted window here and there. No way of pressing charges. Now, if we'd picked him up last night it'd be a different matter.'

It turned out that they'd arrested half a dozen of the likely lads who'd been making whoopee outside the Cadenza, not to mention the three we'd nabbed at the Toreador. Most of them had denied being members of the BUF, but all of them had been armed with hockey sticks, or worse, and Haversham seemed to think there wouldn't be a problem about pressing charges.

And then, all of a sudden, just as Haversham started spooning another couple of sugar lumps into his tea, two things struck me. The first was that I never wanted to see him again. The second was that I'd forgotten to give him the one piece of information that he could really do with.

'Here,' I said, 'you ever come across a chap called Cohen? Tallish? Red-coloured moustache?'

Haversham looked interested. 'Harry Cohen that used to run around with Jack Spot? Had him up half a dozen times. Why?'

'Well, it's short odds he's the chap who turned

over the rubber shop in Wardour Street,' I said. And I explained about the trail of grit that had led up to Rathbone Place and the chat we'd had in the entrance hall.

Outside the sky was darkening and the corporation dustcart had moved off towards Regent Street. A tall, sad-looking chap in a smock was riding a trick cycle up and down the pavement with a boy following to work the crowd.

'Good work,' Haversham said again. His eyes had stopped keeling about now and gone dead still. 'I reckon you and me are all square now.' He gave a little grin. 'Leastways until the next time.'

I'd privately resolved that there wasn't going to be a next time, but there didn't seem any need to let him in on this. 'You mean I can stop going to the Black House?'

'Up to you,' Haversham said. He'd lost interest in me now I'd delivered the goods, which was par for the course I seemed to remember. A bit later, when we'd finished our tea, we wandered off back into Soho, past the top end of Carnaby Street where the mouth of the male urinal gaped.

'Here,' Haversham said unexpectedly, 'you need cheering up. Never seen a chap so down in the mouth. Come on!'

And would you believe he grabbed my arm and steered me off down the metalled steps and towards the door marked 'Gents'. Here, as you might imagine, there was one hell of a stink and someone had left a copy of *Boudoir Nights* face up on the porcelain tiles. I was still trying to work out what Haversham was up to when he threw back his head and bawled out at maximum volume: 'Have your notebook at the ready, constable.' And before you could say, 'Where was Moses when the light went out?' the door of the gents flew open and three little blokes in macs and trilby hats sprinted past us up the stairs. One of them was even buttoning up his trousers as he went.

'Never fails,' Haversham said. Somehow he looked even more sinister when he was laughing. 'Oh dear me.' There was a pause. 'Well,' he said, almost benevolently, 'I got to go.'

'So have I.'

'See you then.'

'That's right.'

'Don't go picking up any of them fake ten-bob notes in that pub in Noel Street.'

If he thought he was going to get any cheery salutations from me, he was barking up the wrong tree.

'No, Mr Haversham, I certainly won't,' I said.

The rain was settling in and I hadn't got an overcoat, so I stayed close to the walls and the shop awnings as I walked down Marlborough Street. By rights I should have gone back on the rents in Bateman, asking old Mrs McElligott, who drank like a fish and sometime had bits of the old sardines she fed her cat with hanging like burrs on her stockings, what had happened to last week's twenty-eight bob, but somehow I didn't fancy it. After all, how can you go round collecting rent from a girl you've just seen doing the horizontal charleston with someone else? That was a question that never made it to the agony column of the *Star*. Between you and me I'd had enough of Dean Street, and Sammy saying he was an Ulsterman, and Mrs Wisbeach and her wretched dog, whether or not she'd decamped with Mr Laal, not to mention all the other things I seemed to have landed myself in up to the neck.

The more I thought about it, in fact, the more I reckoned it was time to be making a move. The question was, where? All the way back into Soho I thought about this while the newspaper posters, which were on about some speech Baldwin had made at the Mansion House, turned to pulp and the more I thought about it the more I reckoned it would have to be the Old Lady's. Now the Old Lady and I don't really hit it off, but there were worse places to spend Christmas, I figured, than snug in Tenterden, with the mist coming in off the marshes, and the mingled smell of moth-balls and barley sugar with the Old Lady reading *The Story of San Michele* for the umpteenth time and the electric fire sending out enough heat to stoke a bakery.

I've never been much of a one for coincidence—after all, if you step out for a stroll in Piccadilly it's four to one you'll bump into someone you were at school with coming out of the RA—but, would you believe it, the first things I saw in the entrance hall at Rathbone Place were a couple of envelopes addressed to me. The first one turned out to be from the Old Lady herself. It contained, along with the news that another of her cairn terriers had died and the drains were bad, the astonishing news that Uncle George was quartered on the premises. The Old Lady didn't give much away, but I had the distinct impression, from reading between the lines, that Elsie had given him the order of the bowler hat. Well, that was a turn-up and no mistake. Poor old Uncle George, I thought, remembering the sight of Elsie marauding over the pavement that morning in Ramsgate, so much for marital bliss. On the other hand, if Uncle George had his feet up on the sofa at Tenterden, this meant I couldn't head down that way myself. There was only the one spare room, you see, and even if I slept on a camp bed in the scullery I knew that Uncle George, the Old Lady and yours truly on the same premises would be a sure-fire recipe for disaster.

While I was thinking about this, and about Gladys again, and how she'd let me down, and how women always did the dirty on you in the end, no matter how hard you tried, I tore open the other letter, so absent-mindedly in fact that I didn't register the handwriting. Would you believe, it was from Netta:

Dear James,

I realize that this letter may come as a surprise to you, but I wanted to say how much I enjoyed the poem you sent me, and how pleased I was to receive it.

As you may imagine, life here is very dull, but I have been reading The Good Companions *again, which always cheers me up.*

I hope you are well.
Netta

I was so surprised at this that I absolutely sat down in a heap on the bottom step of the stairs. In some ways it was even queerer than Uncle George coming to rest at the Old Lady's after Elsie had thrown him out. But then Netta, as I knew from bitter experience—I could still see her throwing the engagement ring at me in the theatre queue—was an odd girl altogether. Just then, looking for a fag to calm my nerves, I stuck my hand in my jacket pocket, and there, curiously enough, was the four pound four Sibierski had given me the night before and I hadn't yet handed over to Sammy. It hadn't been in my hand a second before I worked out what I was going to do with it. After all, Sammy owed me a week's money. I'd take the train up to Auchtermuchty, go and find Netta and see if we couldn't patch things up again. The more I thought about it the more of a tip-top notion it became. In my mind's eye I could see myself walking up the drive of her aunt's house, and the taxi I'd chartered driving off in the direction of the station, and the thump of my suitcase as I chucked it down on the step. Above all, I could see the telegram I was going to send: RECEIVED YOUR LETTER: ARRIVING TOMORROW: ALL LOVE JAMES. What girl in her right mind could resist a message like that, eh?

And so I sat there for a minute or two, smelling the kipper-stink as it floated up from Lew Levy's caff and the diesel fumes from the Post Office lorries, thinking about Gladys and her white legs quivering on the sofa, and Mosley and the Prince, and Davenport's face as he stepped out of the pub in Shaftesbury Avenue, and lying in the cell at West End Central, and the hank of butter-muslin sticking out of Mr Laal's trouser pocket as he sprawled on the carpet in Meard Street, and wondered— something I quite often used to think about—what exactly it was that women wanted. Did they do what they did to you deliberately, or was it part of some bigger thing they were caught up in that they didn't understand? Did they want power? And if they did, what was the kind of power they wanted? And if you managed to work out what sort of power it was, what were you supposed to do about it?

After that I went out to send the telegram.

THE BALLAD OF SOHO

Miss Jones stalks up from Berwick Street,
*   handbag in her hand*
Sniffing out the gentlemen, spying out the land
Shirl and Eth in Argyll Place, near the butcher's
*   shop*
On their feet since half past six, perspiring fit to
*   drop.*
Started out in Stepney Green, on a lorry heading
*   west*
Then breakfasted in Holborn, as if you couldn't
*   guess*
Spent the day in Wardour Street, Bateman,
*   Broadwick, Noel*
And the place is full of people, but they haven't
*   seen a soul.*

Plainclothes man in Poland Street, sees the sky
*   get dark*
Sweeps the male urinal, thinks he'll have a lark.
And down the end of Lexington, the Eyetie
*   funerals pass*
With horses' manes dyed purple, and diamonds
*   made of glass*
There are fag ends on the pavement, there are
*   papers on the stand*
Ramsay Mac's in Downing Street, George
*   Formby's at the Grand*
Miss Jones looks in her handbag, but there's only
*   two bob there*
Decides she'll take a breather by the rails in

Soho Square
And Shirl and Eth go smiling by, behind the
    refuse cart
Not wanting to exchange a word with common
    little tarts.

And the Marquis and the Nelly Dean are
    opening up their doors
With beeswax on the tabletops and sawdust on
    the floors
And Guinness adverts staring from the wall
    behind the snug
And nancy-boys by fruit machines, waiting for a
    mug
With Poles, and Czechs and Bulgars, and other
    far-flung races
And fish-eyed lads from Ealing bent on throwing
    over traces
Join men with lofted placards that say the end is
    nigh
And flaring grocers' shopfronts to light up the
    evening sky.

Miss Jones is down in Frith Street now, and back
    on pavement duty
A stake-out in the shadows that does wonders
    for her beauty
And Shirl and Eth are with a chap they met last
    Whitsuntide
Who took them down to Epping for chips and
    fairground rides
A chap who deals in lead, or soap, or tins of
    Fuller's Earth
Or holds the door as people enter Bourne and
    Hollingsworth.

You can stroll your way from Rathbone Place to
Shaftesbury Avenue
You can walk the length of Marlborough Street,
as Miss Jones likes to do
You can spend a month in basement caffs and
buckshee restaurants
And still you won't have navigated Soho's
homes and haunts
You can go and stand in Brewer Street and
watch the long day wane
The drunks chucked out at three o'clock who're
swarming back again
You can listen to the policeman's tread march
down to Leicester Square
And Shirl and Eth will stop and wonder what
you're doing there

Stop and wonder, smile and nod, but not for
very long
For the noise of Soho never was uninterrupted
song
But a shower of sparks, or a slamming door, or a
rousing drunkard's shout
Or a cap in hand by Liberty when the theatre
crowds come out
Or a police car stalled in Brewer Street by a
well-flung orange crate
Lord M. and Miss McGuiver taxi-bound to
Rutland Gate
You can hear the church bells clanging, above
the nightclub queue
They clang for Miss McGuiver, and they clang
for me and you
Clang for Miss Jones in Kingly Street, Shirl and

236

Eth and the others
The violin shop repair man and the Catholic
*   band of brothers*
Clang for us all, and summon us in, with
*   irresistible might*
To the grey-stone steps where we slump and
*   sprawl in the secondhand daylight.*

James Ross, New English Review,
*   November 1933*

ACKNOWLEDGEMENTS

I should like to acknowledge the help of Martin Pugh, *'Hurrah for the Blackshirts!': Fascists and Fascism in Britain Between the Wars* (2005). Thanks to H. D., J. M.-R., Paul Willetts, James Gurbutt and Andreas Campomar.